***"Then you're . . ."* Raider
began with a sour scowl.**

"Frank James, of course," the man announced. "And as long as we're making introductions, what is your real name? I know it isn't Tool."

"It's Jefferson Davis," Raider sneered. "I guess you didn't recognize me without my goatee."

"The name doesn't matter, I guess," James said, snarling. "How about if we just call you 'Pinkerton'?"

SATAN'S BARGAIN

BERKLEY BOOKS, NEW YORK

SATAN'S BARGAIN

A Berkley Book / published by arrangement with
the author

PRINTING HISTORY
Berkley edition / March 1984

ISBN: 0-425-06845-5

A BERKLEY BOOK ® TM 757,375
Berkley Books are published by The Berkley Publishing Group,
200 Madison Avenue, New York, N.Y. 10016.
The name "BERKLEY" and the stylized "B" with design are trademarks
belonging to Berkley Publishing Corporation.

CHAPTER ONE

Glancing over at his partner, Doc Weatherbee noted that Raider was scowling ominously. He looked as if somebody had recently pried his mouth open and poured about half a bottle of Sheik Achmed's Miraculous Sahara Bitterroot Elixir down his gullet. It was a bad sign. It meant Raider didn't have much fuse left to burn.

"Keep a handle on your temper, Rade," Doc warned his partner quietly. "Remember, this is William's case, and our instructions from his old man are to cooperate with him."

"I was just wondering how Billy-boy would look with the lit end of that stogie shoved about six inches up his ass," Raider mumbled. A trace of a grin crossed his features as he added, "He could probably go on smoking the damn

1

thing, 'cause that's where his head is most of the tim
anyway."

Doc caught himself chuckling over the joke, but wa
quick to remove the expression of humor from his face
"It's entirely the wrong time for levity," Doc reminde
Raider. "People will think we're a couple of ghouls if w
start wisecracking in the midst of this devastation. Just loo
at this place, will you."

Indeed, the interior of the Fidelity National Bank of Kar
sas City looked like a battleground, and for a brief time th
day before, it had been just that. Six people had been mas
sacred in the shoot-out that followed the holdup of the ban
less than twenty-four hours before.

The polished mahogany paneling that graced the interic
of the bank was marred by scores of random bullet holes
and all but two of the six-by-eight plate glass windows i
front were shattered. Scattered out on the tile floor nea
where Doc and Raider stood were chalk outlines markin
where four bodies had lain. Each tracing was splotched wit
darkened patches of dried blood. Behind the tellers' cage
were two similar outlines. Even to men like Doc and Raider
seasoned to scenes of violence and bloodshed during thei
careers as operatives for the Pinkerton National Detectiv
Agency, the aftermath of the raid on the Fidelity Nationa
Bank was a sobering sight.

"Okay, here he comes," Doc said, noting that Willian
Pinkerton had turned away from the policeman he was talk
ing to and was starting in their direction. "For God's sake
try to show a little restraint."

"I don't *want* to start any trouble," Raider sulked. "Bu
boss's son or no, you've got a pretty good idea how muc
crap I'm willing to take from that snot-nosed, pin-stripe
little jackass!"

"Yeah, about enough to fill a thimble," Doc grumbled
"But I'm not quite so eager to put my job on the line, s
just let me handle him."

Letting his eyes stray briefly over Raider's slouchy western garb, Doc Weatherbee had to admit that his partner had about as much in common with the jaunty, immaculate son of Allan Pinkerton as a range steer did with a peacock in full plume. The product of a hardscrabble dirt farm in the Arkansas razorback regions, Raider was as common as grass and as rough-edged as sandstone. He embodied all the elegance of a timber wolf and the dangerous unpredictability of a desert sidewinder. Yet for sheer resilience and stubborn loyalty to a friend or a partner, Doc wouldn't have traded his companion for a squad of imperfect imitations.

By contrast, William Pinkerton's tastes ran in the direction of expensive clothing, imported liquor, and East Coast propriety. William was much like Doc Weatherbee himself in those respects, but unlike Doc, William Pinkerton had a pushy, superior manner about him that grated on Raider's ruggedly independent nature like a nail on slate. Billy-boy, as many of the agents tended to refer to him behind his back, struggled constantly to gain that same fearful respect which most of the company operatives bestowed on his father, but often his efforts came out simply ludicrous and unnecessarily domineering. He just couldn't make the earth shake like his old man could.

"Welcome, gentlemen," William Pinkerton said, shaking both of their hands with an affectedly firm grip. "I've got a tough one on my hands here, and I can put the two of you to good use now that you've finally arrived."

"We left Wichita as soon as we got the telegram from your father in Chicago," Doc explained. "But there was some sort of problem on the tracks, and the train we were on was diverted through Junction City. It cost us about four hours."

"What have you got so far?" Raider asked, growing impatient with the necessity to explain their tardiness.

"I've been interviewing employees and witnesses since yesterday afternoon," William began, "and here's what I've pieced together. There were nine of them, and from the way they handled things, they really knew their business. Four stayed outside, two holding the horses down an alley, and two more by the front door, while the other five came inside. They got the drop on all the customers and employees inside, then passed out flour sacks for the tellers to empty their cash drawers into. The take was something in the neighborhood of seventy thousand dollars."

"What about the vault?" Doc asked. The massive door to the Fidelity National vault was closed and appeared to be undamaged.

"They gunned down the manager, a man named Hiram Coulson, because he refused to open it for them. But that was a mistake. The shot alerted people on the street and the alarm went out. Within a short time all hell broke loose."

"That pretty much goes without saying," Doc noted, glancing around the bank once more.

"At first they tried to get out the front way," William continued, "using people in the bank as shields. But when that didn't work, they bolted out a back door, got to their horses, and rode out. If they suffered any casualties, they carried them along."

"So all the people who died here were either customers or worked for the bank," Doc said.

"That's right. Six dead and nine wounded, including five city policemen. It was a real bloodbath. Headquarters has assigned eight operatives including me to the case."

"So many?" Doc asked. The general practice was to put no more than four operatives on even the major investigations, and two was the more common number assigned.

"Bertrand Walker, chairman of the board of directors for the Fidelity National Bank, is a longtime friend of my father's," William Pinkerton explained. "And besides that, this particular case has one more aspect which makes it merit special attention from the agency."

"What's that?" Doc asked.

"I am reasonably certain that the James Gang committed the robbery," William announced soberly. "This case stinks of their work in a dozen different ways."

Doc and Raider exchanged glances, knowing that no more justification was needed for any extraordinary efforts that Pinkerton might decide to make in this case.

Frank and Jesse James, along with several comrades suspected of helping them in their various train and bank holdups, had been infuriating thorns in the side of the Pinkerton Agency for years now.

The Pinkertons were first called in to track the James brothers following the robbery of the bank at Corydon, Iowa, in 1871, but since that time they had also been placed on retainer by some of the railroad companies that had been victimized by the outlaw band. At least three Pinkerton operatives had died at the hands of the James brothers or their known associates, the Younger brothers, and other operatives and informants who attempted to detect their comings and goings throughout northwest Missouri had simply disappeared. Since before the war, this portion of the state had been home turf for all the members of the gang, and there was simply no effective way that the agency could counteract the widespread local support the outlaws received.

By far the most embarrassing and scandalous event in the long rivalry had occurred in January, 1875 when a band of Pinkertons and local recruits attempted to raid the home of Jesse and Frank's mother and stepfather near Kearney while the two outlaws were believed to be staying there. Two flares were thrown in to light up the interior of the house, but one malfunctioned and exploded, maiming Mrs. Samuels and killing her nine-year-old son. Later it was necessary to amputate Mrs. Samuels' right hand.

Neither of the James boys was captured, or even seen, during the raid. The resulting furor over the bungled attempt by the Pinkertons sullied the name of the agency in newspapers and the halls of government from coast to coast. Attempting to capture known outlaws and killers was one thing, but mangling old women and murdering children in the process was quite another.

But equally serious was the fact that the incident transformed the rivalry between the James Gang and the Pinkerton National Detective Agency into a bitter blood feud. The operatives had always realized that they were dealing with desperate men, skilled and ruthless when it came to a matter of their own survival. But after 1875 there was an added risk in any operation against the members of the James Gang because the matter of vengeance now played an important role. Any Pinkerton who found himself at the mercy of Frank or Jesse James could expect no quarter. Death was a granite certainty.

Letting his eyes travel over the chalk outlines again, Doc Weatherbee was compelled to note, "The James Gang has never been known to create this kind of carnage before. I'm not doubting your word, William, but the files on this gang indicate that they're usually pretty scrupulous about not endangering the lives of innocent bystanders unless it's absolutely necessary. The only common exceptions have been when they were settling old scores or when their lives were directly threatened by someone."

William Pinkerton bristled noticeably at the possibility that his suppositions were being questioned. That was one of the things that prevented him from being a top-notch operative. He hated his word to be questioned and despised being wrong. "There's little doubt that it was the James Gang," he insisted loftily. "And as far as the revenge motive is concerned, you might take note of the fact that Bertrand Walker was in command of a Union regiment during the war, and Hiram Coulson, the man who was killed for not opening the vault, was a member of one of the militia units that tracked the Youngers on two separate occasions."

"But William..." Doc replied, trying to consider the

aspects of the case in his usual methodical manner. It was a lost cause.

"But nothing, Weatherbee!" William Pinkerton interrupted him irritably. "It was the James Gang without a doubt, and this time they're not going to slip through our fingers. I've got the manpower assembled, I've got the full support of local law enforcement, and I've got the logistics available. I'm prepared to track them into hell if necessary."

"That's where the trail's likely to lead," Raider noted sourly.

"We're ready for them this time," Pinkerton claimed. "At this very minute there's a special train being assembled on a siding nearby to carry our party into Clay County, and twenty men are standing by, waiting to load their mounts into freight cars."

"Who are the other operatives and where are they now?" Doc asked. Considering the single-minded zeal of their leader, he thought it would be reassuring to know that a few cooler heads would be along in the event of a confrontation with the outlaws.

"Leon and Paul Fanchette are at the train depot making final arrangements," William said. "Cy Schwartz and Walter Tyndall are over at Police Headquarters interviewing some of the officers who are familiar with the area we're going into, and I've sent Peter Manola on ahead into Clay County."

"You did what?" Raider exploded, unable to control his temper following that final revelation.

"Rade . . ." Doc said, trying to restrain his partner's outburst. It did about as much good as pissing on a prairie fire.

"Don't 'Rade' me, Doc!" Raider growled furiously. "Don't you realize what's he's done? If the James Gang did all this, and if they hightailed it back into Clay County after, then sending one man in ahead of the main bunch is just plain *crazy!*"

William Pinkerton was stunned by the challenge to his

judgment. "I instructed Manola to travel in disguise and to make only discreet inquiries as to the whereabouts of the gang," he explained. "He was told not to undertake any independent action under any circumstances."

"Oh, that's great! That's just fucking great, Willie-boy!" Raider stormed. "I'd say the chances are pretty damn good that Manola will get himself discreetly gut-shot and dumped in a ditch somewhere. Jesus! Don't you know nothing, sonny? That's how much they think of our kind up there in James country!"

Doc could see Pinkerton's fury increasing with every additional word that came out of Raider's mouth, but he knew that at this point he was powerless to stop the rumble from becoming a full-blown earthquake. And William's anger was only increased by the uncertainty that Raider's outburst must have planted in his mind. Sending a man ahead by himself into Clay County was a classic mistake, and one that was likely to cost Peter Manola his life, just as Raider had said. Doc was sure the step could not have been approved by the Chicago office. In his cocksure eagerness, William must have decided on his own to do it.

"If you don't like the way I'm managing this case, you can just get out!" William shouted at Raider. "You heard me. *Get out!* I won't have you working under me. Not now and not ever again!"

"Well, at least you finally got one thing straight," Raider growled back at him. "I won't work for a turd-head that sends his men out on suicide missions, boss's son or no!"

Doc was braced, ready to throw himself between the two men if necessary. He knew that to his partner, anger and violence were two sides of the same coin. Rarely did one occur without the other. But this time Raider somehow managed to restrain himself, though his fists were clenched and his dark eyes were aflame. In the heat of the moment, Pinkerton probably didn't realize how close he was to having his face rearranged.

"Get out!" William screamed at the top of his lungs. Heads turned toward them from all around the bank, and a couple of the city policemen even dropped their hands uncertainly to the hilts of their revolvers. Pinkerton's face was red as a beet, and the veins of his neck had transformed to bulging night crawlers.

But his command was unnecessary. In the same instant Raider spun on his heels and marched toward the wide front doors of the bank. Glass from the door's broken panes showered to the floor as he slammed it closed behind him.

"He's fired, Weatherbee!" William Pinkerton exclaimed. "He's finished as a Pinkerton!"

"That's probably true enough," Doc replied calmly. "But it won't be by your hand. We both know your father has never given you that authority." William Pinkerton diverted his gaze to Doc, threatening to redirect his anger, but Doc refused to play the game. Somebody had to keep a level head in the midst of this ridiculous situation. "And besides that, Raider was right," Doc continued. "His delivery might have been lousy, but his point was well taken. You should never have sent an operative into Clay County alone, and I'd be willing to bet a month's pay that you didn't check with headquarters before you did it."

"It was a field decision," William replied defensively. "Dad was already en route here and couldn't be reached."

"And what about Wagner?" Doc asked, pressing the point. "Did you think to check with number two?"

It was obvious by his expression that William was beginning to have serious reservations about what he had done, but Doc knew it would not be like him to ever admit it. He had adopted that characteristic from his father quite successfully. But there was still the matter of Peter Manola's life to be considered, which made Doc begin to operate more tactfully than he would have liked.

"Maybe you could send word to Manola to just back off and not do anything," Doc suggested. "If he's not nosing around and he just stays out of everybody's way, he'll be all right until the main group arrives."

"I don't have any way to reach him," William admitted. "He left in a hurry yesterday afternoon, and his instructions were to wire me here if he learned anything."

"And you haven't heard from him?"

"Not yet."

"Well, you sure can't start sending off any telegrams in the hopes that they might somehow reach him there," Doc said. "That would blast his cover for sure. My suggestion is that you get your group together and leave right away."

"Our plans were to go within a couple of hours anyway," William said.

"Can't you make it sooner? If Manola's in a tight spot, two hours might make all the difference. Get a wire off to Wagner and tell him the situation. Advise him that you're heading out immediately, and if he has any objections, he can get word back to you before you go."

"You may be right, Weatherbee," William said. For him it was an incredible admission. But then he tempered the remark by adding, "And anyway, the sooner I get things rolling, the more chance I've got of catching the gang unawares." It was obvious where the credit would fall if this operation happened to be successful.

"Maybe," Doc said. But he knew it wasn't often that anybody caught the James Gang unawares, and especially not after a big robbery like the one committed here in Kansas City. If the James Gang was in Clay County, and if William Pinkerton's posse had the good fortune to catch up with them, that gunfight would easily rival for explosive intensity the one that had taken place here at the bank the day before.

"By the way, you'll be staying here in Kansas City, Weatherbee," William announced. "Somebody should be on hand to coordinate any future leads that might develop. Sorry you won't be in on the kill, but we all can't be heroes, can we?"

"I suppose not," Doc answered, trying to sound neutral. Actually, Doc was scarcely disappointed by the announcement that he would not be taking part in the raid in Clay County. In his mind he drew a mental picture of twenty mounted men, Pinkertons and volunteers, spending days on an aimless jaunt through the rural countryside northeast of Kansas City. The members of the outlaw band doubtless had a hundred places to hide in, and extracting any information from the people in the area would be like pulling alligator teeth. Even those residents who felt no wartime or family loyalties to the members of the James Gang were too afraid to divulge any information about their county's most infamous native sons.

And besides that, there was still the matter of Raider to be taken care of. No doubt his partner was already standing with his elbows parked on a mahogany bar somewhere, slugging back rotgut and feeling ready to tear the throat out of the first man who uttered the name "Pinkerton" within a fifty-foot radius of him. It wouldn't be easy to draw him back into the fold this time, and the task of getting the fold to accept him might be even more difficult.

But these were problems that could be handled, Doc realized. Two simple facts had always worked in his favor when he was confronted with similar situations in the past, and they still had not altered. Fact one was that, beneath all the tantrums and intolerance and irascibility, Raider liked what he did. Fact two was equally simple. He was good at it, and Allan Pinkerton knew it.

CHAPTER TWO

Doc's first indication that his partner had returned to his hotel room came when he heard the sound of Raider heaving his guts out through the thin lath and plaster partition that separated their rooms. Doc chuckled and continued changing clothes. Raider wouldn't be going anywhere for a while.

A person would think someday Raider would learn, Doc ruminated as he adjusted the tail of his chartreuse silk shirt into the trousers of his gray vicuna suit. Too much strong drink too fast always did this to Raider, but it seemed to be a lesson he was fated to learn over and over throughout his lifetime. Or else, perhaps, he just didn't care. Maybe the opiate effect of several stiff belts was worth the misery he knew he was destined to suffer later. It was just one of the many confusing and contradictory sides to Raider's complex personality, but after seven years of living and working with the man, Doc knew about, and had adjusted to, practically all of them.

In the midst of buttoning his yellow brocade vest, Doc paused and listened to the chesty *"Ahhuuuugh, Ahhuuug, Ahhuuuuuuuuuhhhah"* that signaled the continuing revolt of Raider's insides in the next room. Doc hurriedly adjusted the knot of his black string tie, slipped on his coat, donned his pearl gray derby, and left his room. In the hallway he stopped a passing maid, gave her a dollar, and requested that she bring a pitcher of cold milk to the room next door. Then he went to Raider's door, knocked once, and went in.

Raider was sitting on the edge of the bed, leaning slightly forward and cradling a brass spittoon between his knees. He glanced up at Doc, his features pallid beneath the bronze tint of his skin. "I thought I locked that fucking door," he grumbled.

"Obviously you didn't," Doc said, crossing the room to the window on the far wall and opening it wide. The air in the place was thick with the putrid odor of regurgitated whiskey and vomit.

"Can't a man have any goddamn privacy at all?" Raider growled. He hawked and deposited his clearings in the spittoon in disgust, then set the receptacle on the floor between his feet. "It's embarrassing as hell to have somebody stand around gawking when you're puking your guts out."

"Well, it's not exactly a new sight to me," Doc commented. He crossed to a small table where a pitcher of water sat in a porcelain basin and moistened a small towel with the water. Then he carried the towel over and offered it to Raider.

"Listen, Doc," Raider said, bathing his face with the towel and then dropping it on the floor beside the spittoon. "I ain't in the mood for one of your silly-assed sermons about how rye whiskey and my weak insides don't mix, so just save it. Okay?"

"Okay," Doc agreed. After countless repetitions over the years, Doc was growing as tired of delivering the lecture as Raider was of receiving it.

"I just had to wash the taste of that mush-brained William Pinkerton out of my mouth, and a few doses of straight rye seemed the best way to do it," Raid said. "Holy fucking shit, Doc! Can you believe that asshole? Sending one man in alone to look for the James Gang!"

"I expect his father will have a few choice words to say about that too," Doc commented. "But probably there's no harm done. William and the rest of his assault troops are on their way now, and they should get to Kearney before Peter Manola has time to get into too much trouble."

"But that still don't excuse Willy-boy for doing it."

"No, nor does it excuse you for your silly outburst. Really, Rade. 'Turd-head'? If I couldn't come up with any expletives more colorful than that, I believe I'd give up the practice of insulting people altogether."

"Go to hell, Doc. I got my point across, didn't I?"

"Even that is highly debatable, my friend," Doc noted.

Their exchange was interrupted by a knock on the door. Doc opened it and greeted the maid delivering the pitcher of milk and a glass. The homely, middle-aged woman started into the room, and then hesitated when she caught a whiff of the odor in the place.

"Thank you very much," Doc said, fishing in his pocket for a second coin and handing it to the maid in exchange for the milk. "I wonder if I could ask one more favor of you? We need to get rid of that," he said, indicating the spittoon in front of Raider. "That is, if my partner's through making his deposit."

"She can take it," Raider said tiredly. "I'm all emptied out."

After the maid had gone, carrying her foul burden with her, Doc filled the glass with milk and held it out to Raider.

"I ain't drinking any of that swill," Raider proclaimed.

"Doc, you know I can't even stand the sight of milk, let alone the taste of it. Not when my insides feel like this."

"Drink it, Rade," Doc told him sternly. "You know it calms your stomach down."

"Shee-it!" Raider exclaimed, accepting the glass and forcing down its contents with a grimace.

Unlike his partner, Doc had been very busy since he and Raider had last seen each other in the lobby of the Fidelity National Bank. After accompanying William Pinkerton and the rest of his group to the special train and seeing them off to Clay County, he had made arrangements for his mule and Raider's saddle horse to be stabled near the hotel, and had paid the liveryman extra to take care of his Studebaker wagon and make sure that nobody tampered with its contents. After that he had returned to the hotel to change clothes for dinner, knowing that sooner or later his partner was bound to show up there.

"I wish we were back in Wichita, Doc," Raider complained. He emptied the glass and Doc filled it again. "We had us a nice neat extortion case there, not a bloody fiasco like this one with a addle-headed jackass in charge of making sure things get even more screwed up than they were in the first place."

"But we had things pretty well wrapped up before we left," Doc reminded him. "With the evidence we turned over to the sheriff there, he was sure to get the grand jury indictments, and he certainly didn't need our help to arrest a couple of file clerks in a cattle company."

"But he'll take credit for the whole thing, just like we were never even there," Raider said.

"Maybe, but the real facts are all in the case journal, Rade. Even if nobody else knows, the old man will realize how well we did our jobs," Doc said. Then he added on a more cynical note, "But I'm not sure even that will be enough to counteract that little scene this morning. It's going to take some doing to save your job, partner."

"Save my job?" Raider exploded. "You have got to be out of your fucking mind, Weatherbee! I thought it was all understood when I left the bank. They don't have to fire me, because I fucking quit. I wouldn't sign back on with that half-assed outfit if old Allan Pinkerton himself crawled into this room on his belly and begged me to come back. I wouldn't take the job if they cut off Willie-boy's left ball and fed it to him for what he done."

"I figure the time to make our appeal to the old man is after William has shown his ass good and proper up there in Clay County," Doc suggested, unperturbed by Raider's vehemence. "Then you and I can go to him and—"

"Is there something the matter with your ears, Doc?" Raider exclaimed. "I told you *I quit*."

"Someday somebody's going to take you seriously, Rade," Doc warned.

"Well, it might as well be today, 'cause I mean it this time." Raider rose and peeled out of his puke-splattered shirt, then pulled another out of his saddlebags. The fresh shirt looked equally crumpled, but was at least clean. He went to the basin and washed his face, finger-brushed his teeth, and ran his wet fingers back through his hair, the closest his black locks usually got to a real combing. After that he pulled his clean shirt over his muscular torso, buckled on his Remington .44, and jammed his dusty black Stetson down on top of his head.

All the while Doc stood across the room watching, realizing that further argument was useless until his partner's pressure valve had released enough steam for Raider to again listen to reason. It was a pattern that Doc was well accustomed to, and it was a measure of his incredible patience that he was willing to go through the same routine over and over again for the sake of the best partner and the closest friend he had ever known in his life.

"First I'm going to get myself a steak as big as a coal scoop, and then I'm going to tie into the rowdiest whore in town and pay her double time for her efforts," Raider announced, starting for the door of the room.

"That sounds like a great idea, Rade," Doc told him calmly. "I think I'll come with you. After all, there won't be much for us to do until we either hear from William or the old man hits town from Chicago."

With his hand on the knob, Raider spun on the heels of his Middleton boots and snorted, "Don't start up with me, Doc. I ain't in no mood for it. You're welcome to come along with me while I blow it out a little in the big city, but let's get one thing straight. Tomorrow morning I'm climbing onto my horse and putting my back to Kansas City, the Pinkerton National goddamn Detective Agency, and the whole lot of you. You can tell the old man I'll wire later where to send my pay and my back expense account money."

"I hear there's an excellent steak house only a few blocks from here," Doc said, smiling. "And I'm sure you'll have no trouble locating your other objective."

"No problem there," Raider said as he opened the door. "I'll just stop the first man I see and ask him where's the best place in town for a man to get a piece of aaaa . . ." His voice trailed off as his eyes set on something in the hall just out of Doc's line of sight.

"Excuse me, please," a female voice said nervously from out in the hall. "I think I must have the wrong room. I was looking for a Dr. Weatherbee."

For an instant Raider was too flustered to even reply, but he swung the door open so that Doc and the young woman in the hall were able to catch sight of one another.

Doc could not prevent a grin of amusement from spreading across his face as he advanced to the doorway. "You're in the right place, miss. I'm Doc Weatherbee," Doc said as he removed his derby and nodded graciously to the new arrival. "I must apologize for my partner's remarks, but I'm sure he had no idea you were so nearby."

"Well, I could recommend someplace to him, I suppose," the young woman said, her brown eyes twinkling.

"Oh, no, ma'am. No, ma'am," Raider mumbled as he snatched his Stetson from his head. "I won't have no trouble... I mean... I wouldn't think of asking..."

"Please, let's just forget the whole thing," the young woman told him lightly. "I know you meant no offense, and none was taken." Then, turning to Doc, she asked, "Are you the Doc Weatherbee who is employed by the Pinkerton Detective Agency?"

"Guilty as charged. And this is my partner, Raider."

"Ex-partner," Raider corrected him.

"And you are?" Doc asked.

"Nellie Rosemond of the Kansas City *Times*," she replied.

"A lady newspaperman?" Raider asked.

"Guilty as charged," Nellie said, smiling up at him. She had a lovely smile that revealed a perfect set of pearly teeth and matching dimples on either cheek. "I'm trying to put together a story on the Fidelity National Bank robbery and I thought you might be able to help me get some of the facts sorted out. It's widely known that the Pinkerton Agency has all but taken over the investigation from the city police department."

"Well, I wouldn't go so far as to say that, Miss Rosemond," Doc told her. "It is true that the agency is helping out, but I'm afraid Raider and I aren't at liberty to discuss the case with reporters. Any information you get would have to come from our superiors."

"That's the way it is, ma'am," Raider agreed when her glance fell on him.

"I can see you gentlemen were just about to go out," Nellie said. "But please, couldn't you just spare me a minute of your time? Please?"

Both men were victimized by her brown eyes to the point of admitting her into the room, but Doc still felt compelled to warn her, "We really aren't at liberty to discuss this case with you at all."

"Well, I tried to locate the agent in charge, a man named William Pinkerton," Nellie explained, "but he seems to have left town already. And I might add that the circumstances of his disappearance are pretty confusing. Where did he go?"

"Like I said before, Miss Rosemond..."

"Well, could you at least tell me when he'll be back?"

"I don't even know that," Doc admitted.

"I see," she continued persistently. "Well, how about if we tried this approach. I'll tell you the facts I already have, and all you have to do is simply confirm them."

"No promises," Doc replied amiably.

Referring to a note pad which she took out of a small clutch purse she carried, Nellie Rosemond began going over some of the specifics of the robbery, including the time and place it occurred, the casualty statistics, and the amounts taken. While her eyes were diverted down to the pad, Doc recognized the perfect opportunity to look her over more carefully and saw no reason not to indulge himself. Raider had been doing precisely the same thing since the moment she had arrived.

She was a trim young woman of about twenty-five, dressed and coifed in a manner appropriate to the profession she was in. Her simple muslin skirt and blouse adorned a figure of slim, attractive proportions, and though she seemed to take no special pains to accentuate any of her female attributes, she had a natural, innocent sort of allure about her. She wore her blond hair up in a functional bun, but a couple of thin curls hanging down along either temple were just enough to prevent her hairstyle from looking too severe and businesslike. The features of her face were pretty enough in a challenging sort of way, and her smiles had a way of putting a man at ease without seeming flirtatious.

Doc noted that Raider's eyes, after a cursory journey

over the rest of her, were now fondling the curvature of her breasts with a roguish delight.

"As far as I know," Doc said when she was finished, "all the information you have seems to be common knowledge at this point, so I see no harm in confirming it, if that's what you want."

"Is it also common knowledge that the robbery was committed by Frank and Jesse James and their gang?" Nellie asked.

"That I cannot confirm," Doc said.

"Well, then, tell me this. Is the Pinkerton Agency in any way connected with the special train that left Kansas City about an hour ago?"

"I can't answer that," Doc said.

"Where was the train going?" she probed. "Was William Pinkerton on it and was he headed out to duplicate the raid on the James farm in 1875? Please give me *something*, Dr. Weatherbee."

"Pretty or not, you're beginning to be a nuisance, Miss Rosemond," Doc told her at last. "Now, I realize that you're only doing your job, but you have to understand that if I divulged any sensitive information about this case, I'd be putting our jobs on the line."

"Your job," Raider corrected him.

"Whatever," Doc said in exasperation.

With no apparent warning, Nellie Rosemond's aggressive attitude began to dissolve away, and with a distinct sense of dread, Doc realized that the young woman was near the point of tears.

"I'm sorry, gentlemen," she said, her face pouting up preliminary to the cloudburst. "I knew I was handling things all wrong with you, but I've seen the technique work countless times for the male reporters." She dug a lace hankie out of her purse, sniffed daintily, and dabbed at her eyes. Doc felt a wave of helpless guilt come over him. Few things were worse than seeing a woman cry and realizing that you're responsible, even in ridiculous circumstances such as these.

"The fact is that I'm *not* doing my job," Nellie Rosemond explained. "I'm not assigned to this story, and I'm not even an actual reporter for the *Times*. My real job is to write obituaries and garden club news. But I thought if I could get out on my own and come up with an exclusive angle on this bank robbery, then the city editor, Mr. Flaherty, would give me a shot at an honest-to-goodness assignment. You have no idea how difficult it is for a girl to break into the newspaper business, and at times I get so discouraged that I just want to...I feel like..." She lapsed into a fit of soft sobs which made Doc look down at the floor and shuffle his feet nervously.

But Raider seemed less affected by her sudden display of emotion. "Look, it really is too bad about you not getting no breaks and all, Miss Rosemond," he said, his voice on the borderline between sympathy and sternness. "But we've got lives to think about here, and running our mouths just now could jeopardize some of them."

"But I'm not on the side of the outlaws," Nellie protested. "I'm not on anybody's side, as a matter of fact. I just want to get my hands on a different angle to this story that no other reporter in town has."

"But what if we told you what our people are doing and where they are?" Raider asked. Doc could not help but note the use of the word "our" with a sense of satisfaction. "You print it in the newspaper, and half a day later a member of the gang that robbed the bank picks up the paper and reads your story. That sorta gives him an advantage, don't you think? He knows where we are and if we're getting close, but we still don't have a clue about him."

"Perhaps," Nellie conceded hesitantly. "But—"

"No 'buts,'" Doc interrupted. "It's nothing personal."

"If you could just give me something," Nellie sniffled. "Anything."

"There oughta be something, Doc," Raider agreed.

Doc Weatherbee considered the matter a moment, then smiled as he came up with an idea. "How about this, Miss Rosemond? If you happened to be at the main depot about one-fifteen tomorrow afternoon, you stand a good chance of meeting a very interesting gentleman who should be arriving in Kansas City about that time."

"Holy Moses, Doc!" Raider exclaimed in alarm. "You mean you're going to sic her on the old man?"

"Or the other way around," Doc said with a grin, "depending on what his temperament is when he arrives. But by all means, Miss Rosemond, don't tell him who leaked his arrival time to you."

"But who will I be looking for?" Nellie asked. "Who's coming in on the one-fifteen?"

"Use your imagination, young lady," Doc said. "We are Pinkerton operatives, and this happens to be a major case for the agency."

"You mean..."

"I mean this could be the break you're looking for if you handle everything properly," Doc said. "But it still won't be any easy task to get your story. I can guarantee you that."

Nellie Rosemond was so delighted with the lead that for a moment Doc thought she might throw her arms around his neck and kiss him, a gesture of gratitude that he would have been hard put to turn down. But instead she clasped his hand in an enthusiastic handshake, repeated the gesture with Raider, and rushed out of the room as if the train she was to meet were arriving within minutes.

Doc and Raider exchanged amused looks, and as they were leaving the hotel room, Raider commented, "It'll serve the old ball-buster right when she pulls that sob sister routine on him tomorrow."

"Wait a minute, Raider," Doc replied, somewhat alarmed by the comment. "She was really upset in there. That wasn't an act." As they rounded the corner of the hall and started down the stairs to the first floor, he stopped his partner with a hand on his shoulder and repeated, "It wasn't an act . . . was it?" The thought that he could have been so effectively conned by a rank amateur was alarming.

"You're a sucker, Doc," Raider chuckled as he shrugged free and went on.

CHAPTER THREE

The first thing Raider's eyes focused on when he woke was a set of wide, bare buttocks pointed at him from across the room. Their owner was leaning over the chair where he had pitched his clothes the night before, rifling his pockets.

He heard her mutter a low, angry "Damn!" to herself when she discovered there was nothing worth stealing, but the expression of pique was erased from her face when she turned and realized he was awake.

"Too bad, old gal," Raider chuckled. "I guess you'll just have to settle for the five I paid you last night."

"Hey, don't get the wrong idea, cowboy," the woman said hastily. "I was just kinda straightening your things. I mean, I wasn't trying to—"

"Don't worry about it, Betsy."

"That's Becky, damn it," she corrected him.

"Betsy, Becky, whatever," Raider said. "Last night I gave my cash to my partner for safekeeping after I commenced to get a load on. All I kept was the five I used to hire you. But go ahead and look if you wanta."

"I already did," she announced with resignation, coming over to sit on the edge of the bed as she spoke. "Look, it ain't nothing personal, cowboy . . ."

"That's Raider."

"Well, it ain't nothing personal, Raider. It's just that on an average Friday night like last night, I can generally go with five or six men and make maybe eighteen or twenty dollars if I try hard. But you were the first guy I met up with last night, and I didn't have any idea it would be an all-nighter."

"It takes time to do some things right." Raider grinned. "Hell, you didn't seem to be in no hurry to cut out of here after we got started."

"I forget I'm in the business sometimes," Becky conceded, permitting a smile to soften the features of her face.

Raider doubted that. This one was no amateur at her trade, or if she was, she'd been giving it away for a good long time before she made it her occupation. Here in the second-floor room of the boardinghouse where she lived, they'd had themselves one rollicking good time after another before collapsing into exhausted sleep sometime past midnight.

Now, in the direct, uncomplimentary light of day, Raider thought Becky still looked pretty good. There were a few signs of encroaching age—distinct crows's-feet at the corners of her eyes, breasts that no longer stood quite so high and proud as they probably once had, a pocking of the flesh across the fatty parts of her legs and ass—but those things hardly mattered to Raider. Experience had taught him that what counted more was what went on after the lights were out and a woman's physical beauty, or lack of it, was cloaked in darkness.

Raider snaked a hand out from beneath the sheet and tickled the thick black muff between Becky's legs, signaling his desire to start the morning off in the same way that they had ended the previous evening. He had already learned she was pretty sensitive there, and he wasn't surprised when she shoved his hand away. But still he wouldn't permit her to rise and move away from him; he held her gentle prisoner with a grip on one of her wrists.

"I'd say you got five dollars' worth of twitch last night," Becky said. "You can't say I didn't give you your money's worth."

"I don't hardly have the matter of fair value on my mind," Raider admitted, pulling insistently on her arm until she lay across him on the bed. "The fact is, I almost always wake up horny in the morning."

"I think your kind drops into the world that way," Becky complained. But despite her protests, her hand was already roving down toward the place where his prod was turning the sheet into a small tent below his waist.

Being in the business she was in, Becky was not used to a lot of preliminaries, a fact that suited Raider fine. Within a moment they had tusseled the annoying sheet aside and Becky was on her knees above him, massaging the head of his thick cock against the sensitive lips of her quim to ready herself for action. Raider reached up to cup her bulbous breasts in his hands, encouraging her bullet-sized nipples into firmness with his palms. Becky closed her eyes and smiled broadly, highlighting the gap between her two front teeth.

Then she slowly descended onto him.

Becky's quim was tight and none too moist at first, but from some magic source inside an abundance of lotiony female wetness soon flowed. In a moment she was as slippery and accommodating as a fistful of butter.

From the start, the knocking on the door was loud and insistent. Raider threw a startled glance over at the door, but relaxed when he saw that the key was still in the hole and the lock was turned. Becky's glance had followed his own, but he saw in her face that her concentration had been broken. Damn, he cursed to himself. A woman's mood could slip away like that sometimes, just like a puff of smoke in a gust of wind.

"I got to see who that is," she told him.

"To hell with 'em," Raider suggested.

"It might be a customer...a paying customer. I got regulars, you know."

"If it is, he'll come back, for chrissake!" Raider said. "If anybody would understand that you can't be interrupted in the middle of something, it ought to be another man that's come for the same damn thing!" He emphasized his point with a thrust of his cock.

She moaned and looked for a moment like she might get back in the mood.

The knocking sounded again, and a muffled voice called out, "Rade, are you in there?"

"I don't believe it!" Raider roared. *"I just don't fucking believe it!"*

"Come on, Raider. Open up. I need to talk to you."

"Is that a friend of yours out there?" Becky frowned at him. "Listen, cowboy, I don't go in for no weird threesome stuff, if that's what you got in mind." She rose up off him and deftly hopped out of bed, leaving his prod standing up like a disappointed orphan. It looked kind of pitiful to Raider, so suddenly and tragically exposed.

Becky pulled on a frayed cotton dressing gown as Raider swung to his feet. He bothered with no such refinements. He stomped to the door and turned the key.

"Doc, I'm gonna kill you," Raider growled as he flung the door open.

Standing in the hallway, Doc Weatherbee looked his

partner up and down. "Well, I don't know what weapon you intend to use," he said, easing past Raider into the room. "but if you plan to flog me to death, I suggest you get to it. It looks like your club is about to go into retirement."

"I mean it, Doc," Raider warned him darkly. "You're a dead man."

"Look, do what you think you've got to, cowboy," Becky said nervously from the far side of the bed, "but just don't do it in my room. Okay? My landlady's none too happy about what goes on in here at night anyway, and if you two start roughhousing, I'll be kicked out on my moneymaker before the sun sets."

"All right," Raider promised angrily. "I'll get dressed and then I'll take him out in the street and kill him."

"It would be a good idea if you covered yourself," Doc suggested calmly. "Somehow it doesn't seem quite proper to be tromping around naked with a lady present."

"You son of a bitch, you know damn well that she's why I'm naked."

"Well, be that as it may, I still feel that—"

"I think what I'll do is I'll beat you to death, Doc," Raider interrupted. "I could shoot you, but then it'd be over so quick I wouldn't get the proper dose of satisfaction out of it." He crossed to the chair where his clothes were and began pulling them on.

"Look, Rade, you know I'd *never* interrupt a thing like this unless it was important."

"You're so full of shit you could fertilize half the state of Missouri, Doc. You love doing this kind of thing. I think you'd rather barge in on me when I'm getting laid than knock off a piece yourself."

"Well, I wouldn't go so far as to say that, but you do put on quite a show at times like this," Doc chuckled.

"Just keep it up, asshole. Make all the jokes you want, 'cause in about two minutes, I'm fixing to wipe that smirk off your face with the butt of this forty-four."

"I've got a new lead in the case, Rade," Doc said. "It has possibilities, and I want to discuss it with you."

"I don't care about that shit anymore," Raider said. He swung his gunbelt around his waist and closed the buckle, then sat down on the edge of the bed to pull on his boots. It was first things first with a man like him. "How did you find me here anyway?"

"It wasn't that difficult," Doc told him. "We're detectives, remember?"

"I'm an ex-detective, and you're a wiseass with a damned sick sense of humor. Have you got any money on you?"

Doc checked his trousers pocket and produced a few coins amounting to something over three dollars. "I left most of my money in the wagon."

"Give it to her," Raider instructed.

Becky accepted the money, but after seeing how little it was, she reminded Raider, "I coulda made maybe twenty dollars last night, except I hooked up with you."

"I guess we both got screwed then," Raider noted as he went out the door. With a tip of his derby and a final smile for Becky, Doc followed.

Raider was surprised to find Doc's Studebaker wagon parked on the street in front of the boardinghouse. The broad lettering across its side identified Doc Weatherbee as a vendor of homeopathic medicines, health restorers, etcetera. It was a cover that Doc often used in his work. Judith, Doc's faithful mule, was standing patiently in her traces, and Raider's saddle horse, a jittery gelding he had purchased in Wichita, was tied to the back of the wagon.

"Going somewhere?" Raider asked.

"Just to Westport for the time being," Doc said. "It's a little town about five miles south of here."

"Well, good luck," Raider said. "I think I'll just take my horse and ride on back to the hotel."

"I checked us out of the hotel about an hour ago."

"It's just as well," Raider decided. "The sooner I light out of Kansas City, the better I'll feel anyway."

"Look, Rade, just ride along with me long enough to hear me out, and then if you still want to take off, there won't be anything to stop you. Your saddle and all your gear are inside the wagon.

"All right, I'll ride as far as Westport," Raider said, climbing up onto the wagon seat beside Doc. "Hell, how long could it take us to cover five miles in this rig? Two days, maybe three if we hit bad weather."

Doc let the insult to his preferred form of transportation go by without response. Their debate over the convenience of the wagon and mule versus the speed and mobility of a saddle horse had been going on practically since the day they were first teamed up together. No consensus had ever been reached. None ever would be.

"I got up early and headed down to the bank with my camera this morning," Doc explained, prodding Judith into motion with a simple "Get up" rather than with a slap of the reins, which most drivers would have used. His affection for the animal was such that he hesitated to show her even that slight discourtesy. "William told me that they were going to clean the place up this weekend and try to reopen for business on Monday, so I figured I'd better get as much evidence as possible recorded on film plates."

"Sounds like a good idea," Raider replied with disinterest. He had always refused all efforts on Doc's part to teach him to use the Premo Sr. camera that Doc carried in the wagon as part of his standard equipment. Likewise, he would have no part in the developing of the pictures. For reasons even he himself could not have explained, Raider mistrusted such newfangled contrivances and chemical processes.

"Well, that was just the routine part of my morning," Doc continued. "The really interesting thing is what one of the city policemen told me in casual conversation while I was in the bank. He was talking about the big scare that the robbery has thrown into everybody around here, and he said that one woman down in Westport even claimed that Jesse James stole some horses from her farm."

"It wouldn't have made sense for them to ride that far to the south if they planned to make their getaway into Clay County to the north," Raider reasoned. "There wasn't any posse after them, was there?"

"By the time they got a posse together, the bank robbers were long gone, and there was no way to pick up a trail on the main roads out of town," Doc said. "But everybody just assumed they went north because it's so logical that they would head into a safe area."

"Makes sense to me, Doc."

"But what if they didn't, Rade?" Doc asked. He let the question hang in the air. He was startled when suddenly Raider burst into laughter a moment later.

"Then Billy boy would be shit up a creek," Raider exclaimed with delight. "Damned if it wouldn't be worth sticking around awhile just to hear the explosion when the old man heard about that."

"The situation would have its minor satisfactions," Doc agreed. "But on the more serious side of things, it would mean that the thieves got away without even a hint of pursuit. Now, I'll admit that's not so unusual when the James Gang is involved. I've heard that, as often as not, even large posses of thirty and forty men are afraid to go after them.

"But it could make them cocky, and it could make them careless to get away clean so often, too," Doc went on. "It seems to me that maybe in this case the answers might not be in numbers and sheer firepower, but in a little shrewd deduction."

"Isn't that what you say when you mean guesswork?" Raider asked.

"I mean *logical* guesswork. It's worked for us before."

"Yeah, and it's sent us out on plenty of wild goose chases like the one Billy-boy's on right now, Doc."

"Still, it won't hurt to talk to this woman in Westport," Doc said. "Many a case has been solved because a minor point wasn't overlooked or a seemingly dead-end lead was pursued. And besides," he added, "it's not such a bad morning for a ride in the country air."

"It's not at that, Doc."

Tillie Deadwick was solid country stock, the kind of woman who had been doing her share of hard farm labor since she was five, and the sort that would probably still be plowing, planting, and harvesting her own crops at the age of one hundred. She was a dried cornstalk of a woman, weathered, wrinkled, wizened, and wary. When she leveled the barrel of her Henry rifle at Doc and Raider on the front porch of her shotgun house and told them she would shoot if she had to, they believed her.

"Ma'am, my name is Doc Weatherbee, and this is my partner, Raider," Doc said, keeping his hands hanging limply at his side in deference to the Henry. "If you'll please be very careful with that rifle for a couple of minutes, I'll explain why we're here."

"Josephine here's fixin' to 'splain to you why you're leavin'," the woman replied. Her voice was as brittle as leaves raking across cobblestones. "Time was, I'd of shot you down first an' then tried to figger out who you was, but I reckon I'm gettin' gentler in my old age."

Raider tried to guess to himself how old she might be, then quickly abandoned the task as hopeless. Time and the elements had cured her skin to the leathery pallor of an old saddlebag, and her steel gray hair, pulled back into a bun on the back of her head, looked as thick and as brittle as broom straw. Tension had pulled her lips taut across her crooked, no-account teeth, and her small dark eyes conveyed an ominous threat all their own. Her faded muslin dress sagged shapelessly over a form as gaunt as a wooden scarecrow frame.

But the rifle she held was in mint condition. There wasn't

a speck of dust or a flake of rust on it, and the way it rested in her hands spoke of an undeniable familiarity between woman and weapon.

"Just give me one minute of your time, ma'am," Doc said, "and then if you still want us to leave, we'll leave." It was a line Raider had heard Doc use many times on him but it didn't work on Tillie Deadwick.

"Git!" she commanded.

"All right, we're going. Come on, Doc," Raider said touching his partner's sleeve and indicating that he didn' think the issue was debatable.

They both turned and stepped down off the rickety porch but before they had gone half a dozen paces, Doc said loudly to Raider, "I guess what they said about her was right."

"Hold on there, dude," Tillie called from the porch "What who said about which?"

Doc turned very casually. "I'm referring to what they said about your report of some stolen horses. We were warned before we came out here that there was probably nothing to it."

"Why, what kind of consarned foolishness is that?" Tillie exclaimed angrily. "O' course them horses was stolen, an' right in broad daylight, too. The day 'fore yestiday."

"If that was true, ma'am," Doc told her with exaggerated courtesy, "then it doesn't seem like you would act this way toward the men who are investigating the robbery."

"Is that why you come here? Well, why in the blasted cain didn't you say so?"

"It's why we're here, but I refuse to discuss the matter with the business end of that rifle pointing at me. If you don't care to be more sociable, then we'll consider the matter closed and leave your property at once."

"No, wait. Wait," she said hurriedly. With some reluctance she leaned the rifle against the wall just inside the door and stepped out onto the porch. "I ain't always this edgy, but a body tends to get downright cautious just after she's been paid a visit by none other than Jesse James himself. 'Specially me bein' a widder woman an' all."

Doc and Raider exchanged significant glances at the mention of the notorious outlaw's name. "Please, Mrs. Deadwick, just tell me everything you can recall about the robbery," Doc encouraged her. "Every small detail might help us catch them."

"Well, sir, when he first rode into the yard, I drew down on 'im jes' like I did the two of you," Tillie explained. "But he was a cool customer, thet one. He jes' looks me straight in the eye an' says to me, 'Ol' woman, we need us some horses, an' we're takin' them o' yourn.' I had me two fine saddle horses that I used for a buggy team, plus a busted-down ol' plow horse right over there in that corral by the barn. But I informed him that he wouldn't even need his own horse oncet my Henry got finished with him."

"But you didn't shoot him, I guess," Doc asked.

"We bargained considerable about that," Tillie said. "He allowed as how if I didn't shoot him, then his eight men who was waitin' in the woods yonder wouldn't burn my whole place down on top of me."

"And you took him up on it?"

"I may be old an' crotchety, but I ain't no blamed fool," Tillie snapped. "O' course I backed down an' let 'im have the animals. It beats dyin', don't it? I could see them other hardcases away off in the trees, an' I could see that all of them was armed an' ready to do some mischief to an ol' lady like me. So this feller, he puts bridles on all three o' my horses, an' off he goes."

"You said this man was Jesse James," Raider reminded her. "Did he tell you his name?"

"No he never mentioned no names," Tillie conceded. Then she added hastily, "But I'd bet a pretty penny it was him. I knowed him from the drawin's they've run in the papers sometimes, an' he had that killer look in his eye. I'll tell you, gents, I've half a mind to go up to Kearney an' just tell that boy's mama how her son treats old ladies. I swear, she oughter tan his tail end for how he done me."

"What did he look like?" Doc asked, taking out a small note pad. He took the description down verbatim as Tillie gave it to him.

"Sittin' his saddle," she said, "he seemed like a tall man. Maybe not as tall as you," she told Raider, "but tall still. He had dark hair an' a bushy beard. It warn't easy to tell for shore, but I'd put him about thirty or better. An' like I said before, he had them killer eyes. It was like the man what owned them hadn't never larned what fear was. Thet's the way them eyes of his looked."

After they had gleaned all the facts they could from Tillie Deadwick, Doc and Raider drove the wagon over to the grove where she indicated that the other outlaws had waited for their leader. There had been no rain in the two days since the men had been there, and the area was littered with the tracks of several horses. Raider got down from the wagon seat and examined the area thoroughly. This sort of thing fell within his area of expertise, just as the photography and interviewing were matters that Doc usually handled.

"What do you think?" Doc asked as Raider started back toward the wagon.

"It all fits about the way she told us," Raider admitted. "There's no way to tell exactly how many horses were here, but nine seems about right. If this is the same bunch who held up the bank, my guess is they must have lost some horses somewhere, either in the shoot-out or along the way here. They probably rode double till they were sure they were in the clear, then stopped here to pick up the extra horses they needed."

"It's got to be them, doesn't it, Rade?"

"It hasn't gotta be nothing," Raider said. "But the numbers seem right. If the one at the house said he had eight men with him, that makes our nine owlhoots." Then he added on a grimmer note, "But I don't see what good all this does us. It was two days ago that they were here, and after that much time it'd be damn near impossible to track them on the dirt roads through these parts. Too much other traffic has passed over the same roads since."

"I never proposed to track them," Doc said. "But this does tell us a few things. For one, we can be reasonably certain they didn't go north."

"Too bad for Billy-boy." Raider chuckled.

"Yeah, too bad," Doc agreed. "But aside from that, I've got a theory about this whole thing."

"Oh, brother!"

"Last night while you were otherwise occupied I went over some case files on the James Gang that William left in Kansas City. They made some very interesting reading."

"And . . . ?"

"One thing that caught my attention was that Frank and Jesse James have often used caves to hide in after they've pulled a holdup. The southwestern part of the state is riddled with them. There's one cave in particular called Clemmens Cavern down near Caseyville that they seemed to favor on several occasions. One of our agents who trailed them to it and arrived only a day or so after they left noted in his operative reports that Clemmens Cavern is extremely defensible and that there seemed to be one or more hidden ways in and out besides the main entrance."

"I hate caves," Raider note grimly. "They're damp and dark, and they always smell like batshit. If you've got caves on your mind, I'm glad I'm not on this case anymore."

"Come on, Rade," Doc said with exasperation. He hadn't heard any more of that quitting talk since they'd left Kansas City, and he thought his partner's brief tantrum must have passed. But apparently not.

"Don't 'come on' me, Doc." Raider scowled. "Technically, I'm still supposed to kill you for that little stunt you pulled this morning, so don't push your luck."

Doc rolled his eyes, trying to be patient, but it was

growing increasingly difficult. To his way of thinking, now that they had a lead to follow, it was time to put aside the bullshit and get on with the investigation. The moment had arrived, he decided, for a little straight talk.

"All right, partner," Doc said. "Let's get this thing settled once and for all. I've got to admit that there are a lot of good reasons why you should quit right this minute. Trailing the James Gang is no picnic, and if we do happen to catch up to them, there's a good chance we'll both find our tails in a sling. Also, if you quit, there wouldn't be any more hassles with Allan Pinkerton or his asshole son."

Raider knew his partner must really be getting wound up when he started using foul language. Such a thing was a rarity for Doc Weatherbee.

"You could save face by quitting," Doc continued, "because there's a strong chance you'll be fired anyway when the old man hears about yesterday in the bank. If you quit you'd be a free man, free to go anywhere you want and do anything you want instead of traipsing all over the country with me, risking your hide on impossible missions against suicidal odds."

"You make it sound like I'd be a damned fool to stay on with the agency," Raider grumbled, feeling oddly offended by Doc's line of reasoning.

"I don't think either one of us has ever decided to our own satisfaction that we're not crazy for being in this line of work," Doc said. "But there would be some definite advantages in the two of us continuing to work as a team on this thing too. Just consider the satisfaction there would be in solving it."

"I'd damn near give my left ball to snatch this one out from under Billyboy and hand it to the old man in a neat little package," Raider admitted.

"In addition to the fact that we would be getting some dangerous and notorious criminals out of circulation permanently," Doc pointed out. "And besides that, if we decided to follow up on this lead, we'd be working pretty much on our own until it came time to call in a backup for the final kill."

Doc paused for a moment, still staring at his partner. An embarrassed sort of look came onto his face, and it was one of the few times Raider could ever remember his being at a loss for words. But Doc made his point anyway, somehow managing to communicate that, after all the difficult times and all the danger they had lived through as partners, saving each other's lives on more occasions than either could possibly count, it would be a shame to go their separate ways simply on the basis of Raider's personal dislike for their boss's son.

"You've got to commit, Rade," Doc said at last, speaking in a tone that left no doubt that he was finished trying to persuade, cajole, convince, or coerce. "One way or the other, I need to know for certain."

Raider caught hold of the back of the wagon seat and swung up beside Doc. "Caves, huh?" he grumbled. "They smell like batshit, and I hate 'em."

CHAPTER FOUR

The restaurant was small, grimy, and dim. Despite the darkening evening shadows outside, only a single kerosene lamp burned near the back, vaguely illuminating the six tables in the place. Doc and Raider were the only customers.

When the kitchen door in back opened, Raider glanced over and his eyes scanned up and down the waitress as she brought their plates of food to the table. Her face was round and plain, with drab brownish hair pulled straight back and pinned in a bun behind. But her body was full and firm beneath her blue dress, and there was something luridly appealing about the way she swung her wide rear end when she walked. His taste for her sort of plump, corn-fed country girls dated back to his adolescence in the hills of Arkansas.

"Let's see," she said to Raider. "You get the chitlins. Right?"

"Not on your life," Raider replied. "I'll take that mess of fried rabbit you've got in your other hand."

"I ordered the chitterlings," Doc said, smiling with satisfaction as she set the plate in front of him.

"Okay, I'll get your coffee now," the waitress said, turning back toward the kitchen.

When she was gone, Raider glanced over at Doc's plate and grimaced. "I don't see how you can eat that garbage," he grumbled.

"It's a regional delicacy," Doc said. "I like to sample unusual dishes when I get the chance."

"But shit, Doc! Don't you realize you're eating hog guts? When I was little, Mama always fixed chitlins a day or two after Daddy butchered a hog, and even back then I'd rather take a walloping than eat 'em. You never saw where they came from like I did."

"They have a most unique flavor," Doc commented.

"Do you want to know where that flavor comes from?"

"As a matter of fact, I don't."

The waitress returned with their coffee, then asked, "Anything else you need?"

"I think we're fine," Doc told her, raising his head and giving her his best disarming smile. "Tell me, miss. What's your name?"

"Bertha Ann," she answered.

"That's a lovely name," Doc said. Raider remained silent, realizing that there was a purpose behind Doc's seemingly casual conversation. "My name is Cyrus Pemberton," Doc continued, "and this is my assistant, Mr. Wilton Tool." Raider scowled at his partner. He hated the cover name Doc had picked for him, but it was too late to do anything about it now. That's the way Doc had signed him in on the hotel register the day before.

"Pleased to meetcha," Bertha Ann replied. "We don't get many strangers here in Caseyville."

"We've come here on an expedition of geological significance," Doc informed her. "We hope to do some spelunking to gather data on substrata formations in this region."

"Uh huh," Bertha Ann replied blankly.

"He studies caves," Radier translated. He agreed that Doc's cover as a geologist would be a useful one here in Caseyville, but he thought his partner was overplaying the role a trifle.

"We've got a few of them hereabouts," the waitress confirmed.

"So I understand," Doc said. "I'm hoping to explore a number of them before I leave here, but the one I'm most interested in is called, I believe, Clemmens Cavern. I understand that it might contain a number of revealing formations and strata."

"I never been in it," Bertha Ann told him. It was easy to see that her interest in the subject was minimal.

"But do you know of it?"

"Sure."

"Then perhaps you might give me and Mr. Tool directions on how to get there," Doc suggested.

"Well, the main entrance is out on the old Marney place, down in a big gully kinda," she said. "From here, you'd go—"

"Bertha Ann!"

The curt interruption came from the back of the restaurant near the kitchen door. Raider turned and saw a ponderous middle-aged man standing in the doorway. He wore a splotched apron which might have once been white, and an unlit stub of a cigar protruded from the corner of his mouth. "Get your lazy tail back to work, gal," he commanded. His voice was a deep, irritable rumble.

"I was jus'—" Bertha Ann began.

"You was just standing there flapping your jaw instead of tending to your own affairs," the man said.

"She really wasn't bothering us," Doc assured the man. "As a matter of fact, she was just about to tell me the location of a cave that I'm interested in visiting."

"She don't know about no caves," the man said. "You can't take nothing she says seriously. Hell, she's just barely smart enough to sling hash." After a quick resentful glance in the direction of the man, Bertha Ann turned and went to work clearing a table across the room.

"Then perhaps you could help me," Doc persisted. "I'm sure that Clemmens Cavern is somewhere in this vicinity, and if you could just—"

"I never heard of it, and neither has Bertha Ann," the man said. "If you two can't come in here and eat peaceable like without pestering my hired help with a lot of damned fool questions, then maybe you'd best find someplace else to take your meals." On that defiant note, he turned and reentered the kitchen, giving Doc no chance to respond.

Raider glanced at Doc and shrugged, then picked up a piece of rabbit and went to work on it. He wasn't too surprised by the man's response. The same sort of thing had happened to them repeatedly ever since they arrived in Caseyville by train a day and a half ago. Clemmens Cavern might be a local landmark, but you couldn't prove it by anybody in Caseyville.

Bertha Ann carried a stack of dirty dishes back into the kitchen, depositing them somewhere with an angry clatter. At one point Doc and Raider heard the rumblings of an argument in back, but the voices were too low to be understood. The two Pinkertons finished eating in silence, and when the time came for them to pay their bill, the burly cook came out and took their money. They never saw anything more of Bertha Ann.

"There's a piece of rotten luck," Doc commented once

they reached the street outside the restaurant. "In another minute, she would have told us where that cave is."

They turned right and walked down the main street of Caseyville. Nighttime had arrived, and there were no street lamps. The street was pitch black except for the occasional splotches of light that poured out of the windows of a few buildings.

"It's the damnedest thing, ain't it, Doc?" Raider said. "Seems like everybody in town has put their heads together to keep us from finding out anything about that cave."

"That could be a clue in itself," Doc noted. "They must have some reason for such secrecy."

"I get it," Raider said. "You think maybe they all want to keep us from going out to this cave because they know who's out there?"

"It's a possibility," Doc said. "The agency files indicate that the people in many rural Missouri communities are in sympathy with former Confederate renegades like the James Gang."

"So where does that leave us?" Raider pondered. "Time's a-wasting. The old man's bound to have reached Kansas City by now, and he's going to be wondering what happened to the two men his son left in charge there."

"I've been studying the problem," Doc said. "If we go back without a shred of information to justify our trip down here, it's going to make us look stupid. But if we stick around here another day, a week, or a month, there's no guarantee that anybody will ever tell us how to get to Clemmens Cavern. I guess we could go out on our own and look for it."

"That's a rotten idea, Doc," Raider said. "Have you ever been in any of the caves in this part of the country?"

"I can't say that I have."

"Well, I have, down where I was raised just a hundred or so miles south of here. Sometimes you'll find a little crack in a rock face, maybe a gap a foot wide and four feet high. When you get inside, you might find a cave ten feet deep, or you might wind up in a cavern two hundred feet high and five miles long. We could spend *years* scratching around these hills and still not find what we're looking for."

"So what do you suggest?" Doc asked.

"I ain't in any hurry to get back to Kansas City," Raider admitted. "Not with Billyboy and the old man both there. Maybe if we put in one more day of nosing around, something might turn up."

"It can't hurt, I suppose."

Raider was ready for a drink to settle his supper, but Doc wanted to go to the stable where he had left Judith and his wagon to check on them. They agreed that Raider would pick up a bottle in a small roadhouse called Grady's on the edge of town. Then they would meet back in their hotel rooms for a drink.

"But see if you can't turn up something a little milder than that vitriol we were drinking last night," Doc said. "I'd swear that stuff started dissolving the lining of my stomach before the night was over."

"It's another regional delicacy, Doc." Raider grinned. "You won't find many places outside the Ozarks that can turn out corn whiskey like that."

"Still and all . . ." Doc said. He strolled off into the darkness toward the livery stable.

Raider took his time heading to Grady's, enjoying the quiet and the cool evening air. Including the time it would take Doc to check the wagon and to dote and fawn over Judith for a few minutes, he would be at least half an hour, so Raider saw no need to hurry on his errand.

Caseyville had sprung up at the base of a long, broad valley that ran north and south in the midst of the steep Ozark hills. Perhaps twenty businesses and three times that many homes comprised the town itself, but it was also the hub of commerce for the numerous hardscrabble farms that dotted the hills and isolated valleys for miles around.

It was a remote sort of place, the kind of settlement that existed pretty much to itself and fostered an instinctive distrust of all outsiders. Caseyville's main source of contact with the outside world was the railroad that ran north toward Kansas City and south in the direction of Fayetteville, Arkansas. By following a dubious wagon road that wound up into the hills on either side of the town, a person could travel east to Springfield or west into Kansas.

Half a dozen male faces glanced up from their glasses of beer and whiskey when Raider shoved open the door of Grady's and went in. Whatever conversation had been going on stopped immediately. Raider felt about as welcome as a toothache as he strolled to the plank bar and ordered a drink.

In his own good time, the proprietor plopped a glass down in front of him and sloshed it full from a grimy, unlabeled bottle. The liquor was as clear as water, and Raider mentally braced himself before slugging the drink back. It burned like pepper sauce going down. Tears blurred his vision for a moment, and he stifled the urge to gag. He pointed to the glass, the bartender refilled it, and he repeated the process.

Raider could feel the eyes of the other men there boring into him. Several feet away at a table, a farmer type mumbled something low and bitter to one of his companions and the man grunted in agreement.

"I'll take one more of these, and a bottle of bourbon to carry along," Raider instructed the bartender. The bartender delivered the merchandise, then stood directly in front of him, waiting for him to finish.

"Now don't go trying to talk me into sticking around," Raider told him. "The way you folks whoop it up in this place, if I ever got started I might be here all night."

"You've mistook me for somebody that gives a shit," the bartender told him flatly. "It's two-thirty for the bottle and the three shots of corn."

Raider surveyed the man and decided he could whip him. It would, as a matter of fact, be a distinct pleasure. But that wasn't taking into account the other men there. He plopped three dollars down on the bar and waited for his change. Then he turned and went back out into the night.

Raider had made no more than fifty feet of progress back toward the hotel in the middle of town when the door of Grady's opened behind him, spilling lamplight into the dirt roadway. He glanced around, half expecting to see the party of cronies stomping out after him, but instead only one figure came out. Raider turned and continued on his way, but in a moment the man called out to him.

"Excuse me," the stranger called out. There did not seem to be any anger or antagonism in his voice. Raider stopped and waited for him to catch up. In the dim light shining from one of Grady's windows, Raider saw that the man was dressed in a neat brown suit, and the way his jacket hung indicated that he probably wore a revolver in a hoster underneath. He appeared to be in his mid-thirties, with affable features and an easy manner about him.

"I'm sorry about all that in there," the stranger said.

"It wasn't your doing," Raider said.

"Still, you hadn't done anything to rate that kind of treatment," the man insisted. "It's just the way folks are hereabouts."

"It's no problem. I got what I went after."

"The name's B. J. Woodson," the stranger said, extending his hand. "I'm just a visitor here myself. I sold some horses over in Texas a couple of weeks ago, and I stopped off here on my way back to Tennessee. My sister and her husband work a little homestead a couple of miles out of town. That's the only reason I'm halfway accepted by these people."

"Uh huh," Raider said. He was not even remotely interested in the conversation.

"And your name is Mr. Tool," Woodson continued.

"You're here with a man named Pemberton, who hopes to study some of the local cave formations." When he noticed the puzzled expression on Raider's face, he added, "I know all that because you came into Grady's right when they were discussing the two strangers who had been asking around about Clemmens Cavern."

"We've been asking," Raider said, "but nobody's been answering."

"I'm headed your way," Woodson said. "I'll walk with you a ways and explain a couple of things to you." Raider wasn't sure what to make of all of this as they walked toward the center of town, but he saw no harm in hearing the stranger out.

"You see," Woodson went on, "there's something about Clemmens Cavern that you don't seem to know, and it's not a thing that anybody hereabouts is likely to talk much about."

"And what's that?"

"The talk is that the James Gang sometimes uses Clemmens Cavern as a hideout when they're on the move from one place to another. That's why nobody wants you going out there."

"Well, I'll be dipped in shit!" Raider exclaimed, trying to sound genuinely surprised. "Are they out there now?"

"I couldn't really say," Woodson told him. "But if I was you, I'd be careful all the same."

"That's enough to make a man want to pack his kit and skeedaddle," Raider said. "But if I know Pemberton, I'll bet he won't let that kind of rumor stop him. He sets powerful store in getting a look inside Clemmens Cavern. Tell me, do you know where it's at?"

"I was there once with my brother-in-law," Woodson admitted. "But don't ask me to show you where it is. I've got a wife and two children that might take it personally if I got myself gunned down by the James Gang."

"So that puts us back at the starting line," Raider said.

"Not necessarily," Woodson said. "I know a thing or two about the place, and if you're still crazy enough to want to go out there..."

"Pemberton will be."

"Then I guess I could tell you about the place. But for God's sake, don't let it leak out who told you. And if you get blasted out there, don't forget that I warned you who you might run into."

"You've got yourself a bargain, Mr. Woodson," Raider told him enthusiastically.

As usual, the lobby of the Caseyville Hotel was unattended, and for the next fifteen minutes Woodson was busy sketching out maps for Raider and telling him some of the things he would encounter in Clemmens Cavern.

He explained that there were at least two entrances into the cave. One was fairly easy to find and provided ready access to the huge main chamber of the cave. The other was more difficult to locate and the route from it to the main chamber was treacherous. He advised Raider on a few items he might find useful once he got inside, and repeated his warning about the outlaws.

"The James brothers and the others who ride with them aren't men to be trifled with," Woodson said soberly. "They've been at their profession a long time, and they're still alive because they're so damned good at what they do. If you were a lawman, or especially a Pinkerton, and you told me you were headed into Clemmens Cavern, the only thing I could say is God be with you. But since you're only a couple of men bent on a little exploring..."

"That's all we are," Raider assured him. He had tensed slightly at the mention of the name "Pinkerton," but Woodson hadn't seemed to notice. "It seems like they'd figure out quick enough that he didn't mean them no mischief."

"It seems like," Woodson said, but his voice was not encouraging.

Raider's informant departed as soon as possible, apparently uneasy about spending so much time in the company of such an unpopular visitor in town. Raider pocketed the sketch and climbed the steps to their rooms.

CHAPTER FIVE

Doc took a sip of the tepid whiskey in his glass and grimaced. It was better than the rotgut moonshine Raider had talked him into sampling the night before, but only slightly. Liquor like this could make the idea of going temperance almost appcaling.

"I tell you, Doc," Raider said from his seat across the room, "the thing to do is go ahead right now and wire for a backup."

"And then?"

"And then just sit here on our tails and wait for them to come. If we got the wire off tonight, Billyboy and his army could be here by tomorrow morning, or noon at the latest. Then we shut the back door with two or three riflemen and come in the front like Sherman taking Atlanta."

"And what if the cave is empty?" Doc asked. "The old man's bound to come along if we send off the wire you're suggesting. If we get in there and don't find any outlaws, he'll be wanting to bury you and me in that cave."

"It's a risk," Raider agreed, "but not as bad as the one we'll be taking if we try to force a showdown with the James Gang by ourselves. Then it's certain that damn cave would be our grave." He had risen from his chair and was pacing by now, a sure sign that his temper was rising. Doc frowned, dreading the argument to come.

"I'm not saying we should take them on by ourselves," Doc said. "I'm not particularly fond of the notion of suicide myself. But we should have some kind of hard evidence to go on before we call in the reserves. Now here's my idea. First one of us should—"

"I hate it already," Raider grumbled. "Damn you, Doc. Don't you think I don't know who 'one of us' is?"

Doc continued, unperturbed. "One of us should slip in there and make sure the gang is hiding in the cave, and then we should wire for support. It's the only logical thing to do, and that second entrance into the cavern that your friend was telling us about seems tailor-made for such a purpose."

"Damn it, Doc, I told you I hate caves. *I hate the sons-abitches!* When things start to get all cramped up around me I go plumb crazy. I could come out of that fucking hole a babbling maniac."

"I wonder if anybody would notice the change?" Doc quipped. Raider's scowl showed that he didn't appreciate the joke. "Look, Raider," he continued more seriously. "You're the logical one to go."

"It always seems to work out that way, don't it?"

"Well, you are. You said you've had experience with caves. And besides that, my presence around town would be missed more than yours would. If anybody happened to ask about you, I could easily explain that you quit and left.

But how would you explain your continuing presence in town if I dropped out of sight?"

"I'd just tell them I loved their goddamn chitlins so goddamn much that I decided to settle down here in their goddamn town," Raider fumed. "You do this to me every time, Doc. You've always got a fistful of fucking reasons why it's me that has to stick my neck out while you sit back on your ass and watch the flowers bloom."

Doc sipped his whiskey and waited, knowing that anything he might say was likely to become more fuel for Raider's tirade.

"I've been telling you ever since Westport that I hate caves," Raider stormed on. "After a while I get this panicky feeling in a cave, like when I was a little kid and somebody held me under the covers so I couldn't move. It's one thing I plain out can't stand."

"But these caves are huge, Raider," Doc argued. "That report I read said the main chamber's bigger than a sale barn inside. Surely you'll be able to stand that."

Raider chugged back his glass of bourbon, his second in the last few minutes, Doc noted. When the liquor hit his stomach, he frowned and rubbed at a spot slightly above his belly button. But the twinge of stomach pain didn't stop him from refilling the glass. Doc took it as a sign that they should get back into action again. When things got slow and a case ground to a temporary halt, as this one seemed to have done, Raider always started putting away too much liquor and growing as edgy as a cougar.

"All right, *I'll* check out the cave," Doc conceded at last.

"I oughta let you, just for spite, you bastard," Raider growled.

"I mean it, Rade. Let me have the map that fellow Woodson drew up, and I'll see if I have any questions. The moon should be up late tonight, and I'll strike out then."

"It'd be a real joy to strangle you, Doc. I know your game, damn you."

"If you think it's a game, then call my bluff. Hand the map over."

"Go to hell."

The two of them stared at one another in icy silence for a moment, then Raider said, "I figure I'll strike out on foot, since the entrance is only about three miles out of town. If I got my horse this time of night, the liveryman would be suspicious. But I've got to scare up a few things first, like some candles and a coil of good rope. Woodson said that back way was marked with splotches of paint on the walls, so I don't guess I'll need anything to mark my route. And I guess I'll need a full canteen and a little grub to take along."

"I've got a small folding candle lantern in my wagon," Doc said. "And we ought to be able to scare up something to fashion a rucksack out of."

"All right, goddamn it, let's get to it," Raider said impatiently. "But I swear, Doc, the next time something like this comes up..."

It was Raider's inalienable right to carp and grumble, Doc concluded, especially since he always went ahead and did the job anyway.

An hour later all the necessary items lay spread out on Doc's bed. Raider was busy dipping the tips of a handful of matches in melted wax to waterproof them, while Doc put the finishing touches on an improvised rucksack. They had little trouble in slipping through town and getting what they needed from the back of Doc's wagon.

It was midnight now, and the whole town seemed to be asleep. In another hour the moon would be up and Raider would head out on his mission.

When Doc finished the rucksack, Raider inspected it briefly and then stuffed his assembled gear into it. The two of them had agreed that once everyting was ready, Doc would stay awake while Raider rested briefly.

Both men paused instinctively and listened when they heard light footfalls in the hallway outside the door. The footsteps drew nearer, then paused immediately outside Doc's door. The two of them exchanged glances, and Raider slowly drew his revolver from its holster. The knock on the door was soft and tentative. Raider quickly stuffed the remaining items in the pack, closed the flap, and set it on the floor beside the chair.

A second knock sounded, and Doc answered, "Yes?"

"Dr. Weatherbee? Is that you?" a cautious female voice asked.

The partners frowned at one another. Neither recognized the voice, but they were both immediately aware of the fact that nobody here in Caseyville was supposed to know Doc's real name. As Raider eased around behind the door, still holding his pistol ready, Doc went over and opened it.

"You!" Doc said in amazement as he looked out into the hall.

"It's me all right," the woman answered.

"Well get in here, girl," he said.

Nellie Rosemond entered the room with a soft rustle of skirts, and Doc closed the door hurriedly behind her.

"Well, goddamn!" Raider exclaimed in open disgust as he holstered his weapon and stepped forward. "How in the ever-loving hell did you find us way off down here?"

"It wasn't as difficult as you might imagine," Nellie said, smiling openly at the two men despite their scowls. "It wasn't anything a shrewd reporter couldn't handle easily enough." She set her carpetbag on the floor by the door, then untied the ribbons of her bonnet and took it off.

"So let's hear it, Miss Rosemond," Doc said. "It's important for Raider and me to know how much meddling you've done into our affairs."

"That's not a very nice attitude for you to take," Nellie said. "After all, I have my job to do, just like the two of you."

"But the way you're doing your job could put our necks on the line," Doc said. "Now tell me how you traced us to Caseyville."

"It was amazingly easy," she admitted. "When I discovered that the two of you had checked out of your hotel and left, I just started nosing around at the depots and the stage station. I found out that two men had used Pinkerton passes to board a train in Westport, and the station agent there remembered that they had also loaded a wagon and a mule and a horse onto the train. He also recalled that you had to pay extra for the freight of the wagon and that your destination was Caseyville."

"Damn, Doc," Raider exclaimed. "I didn't think about the train passes giving us away. Did you?"

"I'm afraid I didn't," Doc said.

"So anyway," Nellie continued, "I caught the train in Westport earlier today and arrived here about half an hour ago."

"And then?"

"And then I came here to the hotel, because it seemed the most logical place for you to be staying. There wasn't anybody on duty downstairs, but only two keys were gone from the hook board, so I came on up. When I saw the light on under the door, I came here and knocked, hoping it was your room."

Raider looked at Doc and rolled his eyes. They thought they had been so clever, slipping out of Kansas City and concocting such an elaborate cover story here in Caseyville, and now a novice reporter had blown the whole thing with the kind of deductions that any six-year-old could make. "Are you thinking what I'm thinking?" he asked Doc.

"Probably," Doc said.

"Well, if it involves my putting the two of you in jeopardy, I don't see how I possibly could have," Nellie said defensively. "I haven't talked to a single human being since I stepped off that train thirty minutes ago."

"That's a lucky thing, but it's not exactly what we were referring to," Doc told her. "You see, Raider and I have been using different names and a cover story since we got here, but we haven't gotten much cooperation from anybody in town. All we've run into was suspicion and belligerence. Now it seems likely that if you traced us here with our Pinkerton railroad passes, the local people might have figured out who we are by the same means."

"All it would take was for the conductor on the train to mention who we were to the station agent here in Caseyville," Raider agreed. "Word would have been all over town about us an hour after we got here."

"But what I still don't understand is *why* you're here," Nellie said.

"We can't tell you that," Raider said.

"But if it makes you feel any better," Doc added, "since we've been here, we haven't turned up a thread of evidence that the James Gang is anywhere close about. For all we know, William Pinkerton might already have the whole bunch in custody up there in Clay County."

"Not unless he did it in the last few hours," Nellie said. "Just before I left Kansas City, the word was going around that he and his posse were giving up and heading back."

"Hot damn!" Raider exclaimed. "I bet the old man's burned up about that."

"Among other things," Nellie said with a sly smile.

"Meaning?" Doc asked.

"Yesterday morning I was over at Police Headquarters and I just happened to overhear a piece of a conversation between your employer and the police captain. They were discussing this case, and the door to the office wasn't quite closed. . . . Anyway, Mr. Pinkerton was telling the captain that two of his men were violating all the company's General Principles by launching out on their own and not reporting back where they were or what they were doing."

"He was pretty hot about it, huh?" Raider asked.

"He was using curses I haven't heard for years, and he seemed to be making up a few new ones specifically for the occasion. I made sure I was gone before he came out of there."

"The old man's got a temper," Doc said unnecessarily.

"I sure wouldn't want to be either one of you, the next time you're around him," she said. "Not unless you had something positive to justify your disappearance."

"Well, it's like Doc said. We don't," Raider told her.

"The trip has been fruitless so far," Doc agreed.

"So far?" Nellie asked.

Both men could see that the young reporter was determined to get some kind of story from them, but they were equally determined that she would not. If she happened to get hold of the information about Clemmens Cavern and wired the story back to the *Times,* seven different kinds of hell could break loose as soon as tomorrow's edition began circulating around the countryside. Without even having to discuss the matter, Doc and Raider both knew she would have to be kept in the dark at least long enough for them to check the cave out and call for reinforcements.

"You look tired, Miss Rosemond," Doc said. "You probably won't be able to scare up the hotel clerk tonight, so why don't you sleep in Raider's room next door. He can bunk in here with me for one night."

"It *has* been a long day," Nellie said. There was a glimmer of suspicion in her eyes, as if she sensed that perhaps she was being manipulated. Her eyes roamed the room briefly, then came back to Doc's face. He made sure that his expression revealed nothing.

"Just pitch my gear out of your way," Raider told her, stepping forward to surrender his room key. "The bed ain't much, but it beats sleeping on the floor."

"Thank you very much. I'm sure it will be fine," Nellie said. After a final glance at both their faces, she turned to the door. "Good night to you, gentlemen."

• • •

Traces of moonlight were just beginning to filter through the treetops when Raider headed out an hour later. Once he had cleared the edge of town, he paused to put a candle in Doc's candle lantern and light it. The small glass-sided lantern protected the flame from the nighttime breeze and illuminated the dirt road ahead of him with flickering light. Following the dictates of Woodson's map, he headed due west into the steep Ozark hills.

Along most of the way, the thick forests of oak, pine, and hickory crowded right up to the edge of the roadway, shrouding the route with darkness even as the moon rose higher in the sky. Occasionally he passed open fields of corn and ramshackle farmsteads, carved out of the rugged hillsides by the determined pioneers of the area. From his boyhood days, Raider realized the difficulties of trying to scratch a living from these lovely but inhospitable mountains. No matter how hard folks worked, it wasn't likely that they would ever rise far above subsistence in such a place. It was no wonder, he reflected, that his mother had died young and his father had eventually turned to drunkenness as an escape from his lifelong accumulation of disappointments and despair.

He found the fork in the road that the map indicated and took the less used track to the left. The rock-strewn trail climbed steeply up a hillside, then descended just as abruptly into a valley beyond. At the base of the hill, Raider turned off the road, following a meandering creek that carved its winding route up the valley floor. According to Woodson, this back way into Clemmens Cavern was more than a mile from the main entrance, but the twisting underground course actually measured closer to two miles.

Navigating it was not a task Raider was looking forward to.

At last he located a flat overhang similar to the one Woodson had described to him. It was a shelf of rock about twenty feet long that extended out over the edge of the creek at a height of about two feet. Raider eyed it skeptically for a moment, then got down on his knees in the water and peered underneath. The light from his lantern danced into the dim recesses, revealing little.

"Goddamn," he muttered bitterly to himself. Every nerve in his body was telling him he had no business crawling under there. It was a place suitable for lizards and snakes and other slimy things, not human beings. Despite the brittle cold of the creek water rushing around his legs and feet, a sticky sweat began to coat his upper body. "Goddamn!" he hissed again. He tilted his head beneath the overhang, thrust the lantern out ahead of him, and crawled forward on his hands and knees.

After no more than twenty feet of progress, he paused to look back in the direction he had come. Beyond the range of the candlelight, darkness surrounded him on all sides. A panicky feeling swept over him when he realized he could no longer see the outside world, and he could clearly imagine the terror of being irretrievably lost deep within the stony intestines of the mountains. It was an impossible task. He simply couldn't do it.

But he could explore a few more feet, he decided, just far enough to prove beyond a doubt that it was a challenge beyond his capabilities. The passageway made a sweeping turn to the right, and there he spotted the first marker. It was a circular splotch of white paint on the rough stone wall. When he realized that without a doubt he was in the right place, the strongest feeling he had was one of disappointment. It would have been much simpler to go back and report to his partner that he couldn't find the entrance.

Past the painted blaze, the stone ceiling rose slightly, and soon Raider found that he could stand up and walk, though he had to do so leaning forward awkwardly. The proper route was marked by the same circular marks on the floor about every twenty or thirty feet. His nerves calmed slightly, and he forced from his mind the thought of the layers of rock closing up on him, squashing him like a bug between two anvils.

When the candle in the lantern went out, the darkness swallowed him up suddenly and completely. Never before since childhood had Raider been afraid of the dark. In fact, on countless occasions in dangerous situations he had actually considered the nighttime an ally and a weapon. But until this moment, he had never before experienced *true* darkness.

It was awesome.

Clumsily, with an edge of frenzy to his actions, he fished in his pack for another candle and a match. The relief when the light flickered back to life was akin to true joy. He laughed, a giddy, nervous giggle, and the darkness around him greedily swallowed up the sound.

A few feet ahead an arrow painted on the stone floor marked a change in direction. It pointed to a split in the rock about eight inches wide and three feet high.

"Oh, no, Doc," Raider muttered. "Damn your eyes, I ain't going on in there!"

But it wouldn't hurt to stick his head through and look around, he decided. As he explored the hole with his dim light and his eyes, he saw very little. But he sensed openness beyond. He inched into the hole, holding the lantern in front of him. The passageway funneled open rapidly ahead. He heard a faint sound that could only be the babble of flowing water.

Encouraged by the prospect of open spaces, he squeezed through the narrow opening, holding the lantern out in front and pulling his pack through behind. It was difficult going, and at one point his skull rapped against the ragged stone above his head, opening a gash in his scalp. A trickle of blood flowed down across his left temple into his eye, blurring his vision. He decided the best thing would be to make his way to the water and tend the wound before pushing on. From the sound, it couldn't be far ahead.

He wasn't sure what happened as he brought his feet

clumsily around and started to rise. One minute the stone floor was there firmly beneath him, and the next he was tumbling forward in an avalanche of small stones and rubble. The lantern flew from his hands and went out, and for a time it seemed as if he would roll downward forever, transported on a steep sheet of gravel and rocks to his grave deep in the earth. Rocks the size of a man's head and larger rolled along with him, pummeling and pounding him in dozens of places, and the dust raised by his fall clotted his lungs.

He was dazed and only half conscious by the time he rolled to a stop in the utter darkness. The noise of the flowing water somewhere close by mixed with the clatter of tumbling rocks and refuse that half buried him before it stopped.

"Caves! Shit!" Raider growled as he sat up and freed his legs of the blanket of stone that covered them. He was in the dark again, and half afraid of moving for fear he might start to fall again. He was battered and bloodied from head to foot, and his mouth was filled with acrid-tasting grit. During his fall his pack had torn open and emptied, and it now hung limp and ragged on his back. Its contents were undoubtedly strewn and buried along the entire length of the steep grade he had just unwillingly descended.

Raider sat for a while, just letting his body recover from the fall as his senses started to regroup. The running water sounded invitingly close, but he was afraid to move from the spot where he was lest he get disoriented and lost forever in the blackness. At least right now he knew approximately where his gear was, even if it seemed next to impossible to crawl back up the grade and retrieve it.

He spotted a glimmer of light far up the debris-covered slope. At first he thought the flame in the candle lantern had survived. Perhaps the lantern had fallen on its side and it had taken the candle inside a moment to recover. He raised to a squat and turned, preparing to begin the difficult ascent.

Then the light moved.

It drew closer and brighter, and finally Raider spotted the flame itself. There was a short, surprised yelp, the flame disappeared, and he heard the unmistakable commotion of another body barreling down the discomforting downhill slide.

CHAPTER SIX

When the clatter ended a minute later, Raider located the second victim of the underground hillside by her whimpers. He scrambled through the darkness along the base of the grade for a few feet before reaching out and touching something that he finally identified as a shoulder covered by a torn sleeve.

"Who is it?" she gasped in surprise. Raider recognized Nellie Rosemond's voice.

"Who in blazes do you think it is?" he responded angrily. "Lady, you must have chowder for brains to come off alone into this damn hellhole!"

"I wasn't smart like you, huh?" Nellie groaned, attempting to sit up.

"Well, goddamn!" Raider exclaimed. "At least I had a map to go by."

"And I had a guide," Nellie replied. "Though I'll admit your services leave something to be desired."

"The man that told me about this place didn't say anything about a goddamn underground mountain that you have to fall down to get where you're going," Raider complained.

"Well, at least I had the presence of mind to do something that I bet you didn't," Nellie said.

"And what's that?"

"Just watch," she said, rummaging around in the darkness. In a moment a match hissed to life and touched against a wick. "I held onto my candle," Nellie told him smugly.

"That is something," Raider admitted grudgingly. "But you still haven't told me why you're down here in the first place. What does it take for a man to shake you off his shirttail?"

"That slide almost did it for you," Nellie said. From the look of things, the fall had been pretty rough on her, too. Her cotton shirt and trousers were a ragged shambles, and she was bleeding slightly from half a dozen cuts and scrapes. Her face was sooty brown with dust and her hair was tangled and filthy. But she still had the spunk to give Raider a smile.

"I knew you two were up to something back there in the hotel," she said. "I just had a feeling. When I got to your room, I changed clothes, then I listened at the wall instead of going to bed. Finally, when I heard somebody go out, I waited a minute and then I followed. I didn't even know which one of you it was until you got on down the road and lit that lantern."

"I wish I'd known you were back there," Raider said. "I could have arranged a surprise for you."

"You were easy to follow because of that light," Nellie told him. "I could stay way back so you wouldn't hear me. But I sure wasn't prepared for where you would lead me. It was just a lucky thing I thought to stick a couple of candles and a few matches in my pockets before I left your room."

"Yeah, lucky as hell," Raider grumbled.

"When you went in under that rock, I would have lost you," she continued. "But as I got closer I heard you cursing. That's a pretty bad habit you've got, Raider. Your foul language."

"Well, I've had damned plenty to cuss over since I got in this lousy place," Raider said. "Just look at the mess we're in. Both of us are banged up like a couple of bronc busters, my gear is scattered from here to Jerusalem, and the last marker I saw was way the hell back up at the top of that slope."

"I assume your being in this cave has something to do with the James Gang and the bank robbery," Nellie said. "So what do you plan to do now? Just give up?" Her voice had a note of challenge in it. "I say we push on," she told him. "If we scout around awhile we might find another one of those splotches of paint. They are what we've been following, aren't they?"

"What is this 'we' business?" Raider demanded. "No matter what I decide to do, you're going back. You're going out the same way you came in."

"But Raider . . ." she protested. They both looked back up at the long, cluttered incline they had just slid down. By the scant light of Nellie's candle, neither of them could even see how high it went. Its upper reaches were veiled in darkness.

"First, though, let's find that water I've been hearing and see what we can do about these cuts and things," Raider said.

"I'm for that," Nellie said.

They descended a narrow, treacherous path of sorts for another fifty feet before finally reaching the water. From what they could tell, it was an underground stream that rippled and tumbled across a smooth stone bed about ten feet wide. The water tasted limy, but they risked drinking it and using it on their injuries anyway. The worst wound Raider had was the gash on his head. It stung like the dickens when he examined it with his fingers, but the blood around it was thickening, and the flow had nearly stopped.

"Would you look at a place on my back?" Nellie asked him from a few feet away. "I can't reach it."

As he turned to her, she knelt with her back to him and removed her ragged blouse. Raider picked up the candle, and after she had pulled her camisole over her head, he held the light up to examine the abrasion low in the middle of her back.

"It's just a deep scrape," Raider said, splashing a couple of handfuls of water on the spot to wash some of the cave dust off. "It could use dressing, but it's not too serious."

"It hurts," Nellie said.

"Well, it's gonna," Raider said. "It's what you get for coming in here in the first place."

"Thanks for the sympathy, Raider."

Nellie's camisole was so badly mutilated that she discarded it, then she leaned forward and began rinsing her blouse out in the stream. Sitting as she was, her breasts hung down enticingly below her, and Raider noted that she had more up front than was evident when she was fully dressed. After a moment Nellie glanced around at him, and when she realized what had captured his attention, she turned away. But it was all very casual. She really didn't seem to mind his stare.

"So have you decided?" she asked as she pulled her damp blouse on and buttoned it.

"I've come this far," Raider said. "I might as well see how much of my gear I can round up and then push on. The rest of the way couldn't be much worse than what we've already been through."

"And what about me?" she asked.

"Maybe you'd be better off sticking with me," he admitted grudgingly. "But if you come, it will be on two conditions. One, you do exactly what I say every step of the way from here on. And two, you don't wire any stories back to your paper until Doc and I say it's all right."

"I suppose I can live with that," Nellie agreed. "And since you're going to be cooperative, so will I. Look over to the left, where that piece of rock juts out over the water."

Raider held the candle up and looked where she indicated. In the dim light, he saw a white patch of paint and an arrow pointing the way.

Eventually they discovered that they were in a huge chamber of the cavern. The ceiling stretched up far beyond the reach of the candlelight—at least a hundred feet, Raider estimated. The trail they were following alongside the underground stream moved at a gentle downward angle for nearly half a mile, then started upward again more steeply. At the point where the grade shifted direction, the stream flowed into a split in the rock floor and disappeared.

Raider had recovered most of his equipment, and they had replaced Nellie's uncertain candle with the steadier light of the lantern. With the wide-open spaces around him, Raider calmed down somewhat and regained a sense of purpose.

The sights they passed along the way were truly incredible. Glistening stone columns thirty feet in diameter rose from the cavern floor and disappeared into the darkness above. Their polished, rippled sides were streaked with endless shades of cream, red, pink, and brown. Some formations along the walls had the appearance of miniature white forests stacked one on top of the other, and in other places the stone took the shape of delicate, cascading ribbons. Nellie was fascinated by all of it and kept trying to offer explanations of how this or that formation had come to be. But Raider was only passingly interested. His main concern remained to get the job done and get the hell out.

Eventually, as they neared the upper end of the chamber, the walls began to narrow and the ceiling descended into view. Raider's apprehensions increased accordingly. His mind's eye was once again picturing constrictive passageways and winding, nerve-racking fissures where no sensible person would ever want to go. But none of it seemed to bother Nellie Rosemond in the slightest, and so he felt compelled to keep all the tension bottled up.

At the top of the chamber, they passed into a tunnel of sorts. The floor was littered with fractured hunks of stone that had fallen at various times from the ceiling, but only a couple of places were tight enough to cause them any problems. The paint marks and arrows occurred frequently enough to assure them that they were still heading in the right direction.

Along the way, Raider gave Nellie some of the details of why he was here and what he hoped to see at the other end of the cavern. He saw no harm in taking her into his confidence at this point, and his only hope was that she wouldn't betray the faith he was putting in her. Despite her conniving and her irritating zeal, he felt he could trust her.

As the passageway they were in began to widen again, Raider paused and halted Nellie with a hand on her arm.

"What is it?" she asked. "Did you hear something?"

"No, but I might have smelled something," Raider said. "For just a second there, I thought I caught a whiff of wood smoke."

"You mean...?" Nellie asked. "Could we be getting close to where they are?"

"It's possible. I don't know how far we've come, but it seems like miles. It could have been far enough."

"Oh, Raider! The James Gang!" she said in quiet awe. She edged closer to him until her arm was touching his, and she reached out to touch his hand, as if for reassurance.

"I guess we won't know for sure until we get close and have a look, but from here on we'll have to stay quiet. I think I'll put the lantern out and just carry a candle in case we have to put it out in a hurry."

"I'll do everything you say," Nellie assured him. She was

trembling slightly, either from excitement or fear.

The progress was slow from there on. Raider chose every step carefully, and paused often to listen and test the air. The scent of wood smoke increased, and soon Raider heard the sound of cascading water. Somewhere ahead was an underground waterfall, he decided.

When the tunnel finally opened into what appeared to be another enormous chamber, Raider extinguished the candle. Working in the darkness, he cut the flap from his pack and fashioned a sheath for the candle lantern, leaving only a tiny hole on one side for the light to come out. That would have to suffice from here on.

They continued to inch forward, crossing an area of jumbled stone and rubble. When they had moved as close as they dared, they knelt behind a waist-high boulder to study the territory ahead. The bonfire was about a hundred feet away from them across an open, rock-strewn stretch of ground. It had been built along the edge of a broad level portion of the cave floor, and its flames lit the entire area.

On the opposite side of the large chamber, at least fifty feet from the fire, a sheet of water cascaded from a slit about fifty feet above the cave floor, forming a pale, shimmering waterfall. A broad, lovely pool had been formed at its base, and at one edge of the pool the water overflowed into a canal and down a shadowy passageway.

A single figure knelt by the fire with his back to Raider and Nellie, tending a piece of meat that was roasting over the flames.

"Shouldn't there be more than one of them?" Nellie asked in a whisper. "One man is not much of a gang."

"They might have split up, or there might be more of them farther along in the cave where we can't see them," Raider said. "I wish I knew, because if he's by himself, I could take him easy enough."

"He might not even be part of the gang," Nellie suggested.

"Maybe not, but I wouldn't worry about that until I had

the drop on him. But I'd better not risk it. If something went wrong, it would mess up the whole plan."

The faint scrape of a shoe on loose gravel behind them alerted Raider to danger. He tensed himself to spin, draw, and fire, but the metallic sound of a lever-action rifle being cocked made him freeze instead.

"I wouldn't," a stern female voice advised.

The man beside the fire rose and turned as Raider and Nellie's youthful captor ordered them to march forward. As they neared him, he said with a smug grin, "Welcome to Clemmens Cavern, Mr. Tool, or whatever your name is. I didn't expect you to bring a female companion along."

"Damn you, Woodson," Raider snarled. "You can't draw a map for shit. What's this all about?"

"It's a trap," the man announced, casually drawing his revolver from the holster under his jacket. Then he said to the young woman who stood to one side, still threatening them with her Winchester, "I can cover them, Lucy. You run outside and tell Jesse our visitor has arrived." The young woman turned and moved into the darkness.

"We had Lucy hiding in the rocks back there in case you decided to come that way, and my brother was guarding the main entrance," he explained. "I was the bait."

"Then you're . . ." Raider began with a sour scowl.

"Frank James, of course," the man announced. "And as long as we're making introductions, what is your real name? I know it isn't Tool."

"It's Jefferson Davis. I guess you didn't recognize me without my goatee."

"The name doesn't matter, I guess," James said. "How about if we just call you 'Pinkerton'?"

Nellie glanced up at Raider, clearly worried that the outlaw knew his identity, but Raider tried to show no trace of alarm.

"Look, James, the young lady here's really not with me,"

Raider said. "She's just a nosy goddamn reporter that followed me in here. She can't do you no harm."

"A reporter," James said. "That's interesting. It looks like you and your partner didn't do such a good job of keeping your true identities secret."

"We might as well have worn signs," Raider admitted with disgust.

In a few minutes Lucy returned from the front of the cave, bringing another man with her. So this was the second half of the famous duo, Raider thought as he appraised the new arrival.

On first glance, Jesse James looked ordinary enough. He stood about six feet tall, a couple of inches shorter than Raider, and like his brother he wore a neat dark suit. A black beard covered the lower portion of his face, and there was nothing distinctive about his features.

But when he drew his revolver and pointed it at Raider's midsection, a strange change came over his face. It was like the man behind it had turned to stone. "I'll see you in hell, Pink," he said as he thumbed the hammer back. Nellie gasped in shock and Raider braced himself to die.

"Don't kill him just yet," Frank said as calmly as if he was asking his brother to pass the biscuits.

"The bastard's a Pinkerton, Frank," Jessie stormed. "They killed our little brother and crippled our mother with their goddamn stupid sneak attack. And now you don't want me to kill him? Isn't that why we got him here?"

"Yes, of course," Frank conceded. "But we don't have to do it this very minute. For all we know, they might have a whole army headed this way by now, and for the time being he might be more use to us alive."

"Shit!" Jessie exclaimed in disgust. His revolver was still cocked, still pointed at Raider's gut. A belly wound was an ugly thing, a slow, painful way to die. "Holding a prisoner is a pain in the ass, Frank," Jesse complained, still pitching for an immediate execution.

"Then let's just fix him so he won't be any trouble," Frank said. As he turned back toward Raider, he brought the barrel of his revolver up, crashing it against the side of Raider's head. For Raider the world went as black as the most remote corner of Clemmens Cavern. He crumpled to the ground.

CHAPTER SEVEN

Raider's head throbbed. Strong rope bound his hands and feet. His throat was parched, and his mouth was filled with the acrid taste of cave dust. But worse than any of the physical discomforts was the stark realization of what a desperate situation he was in. He wasn't fool enough to hope for any sort of mercy from Frank and Jesse James.

He lay on the hard stone floor, facing the fire. At first there seemed to be no one else around, but trussed up as he was and lying on his side, it was hard to tell for sure. He was concerned for Nellie's safety. Although her fate wasn't as tightly sealed as his seemed to be, she was still by no means safe. The James brothers had no known history of killing women, but if it was necessary, he had no doubts that they would do so.

At last he rolled over onto his back and then on his other side to get a look at the rest of the cave. It was then that he realized he was not as alone as he had believed. Over in the pool at the base of the underground waterfall, his original captor, Lucy, was bathing.

In the heat of the moment when he and Nellie were first taken prisoner, he had not paid much attention to Lucy except to note that she was young and seemed threateningly familiar with the rifle she wielded. But now suddenly he had the chance to study her in a much more intimate way than he would ever have expected. Believing him to be still unconscious, she was enjoying the water with uninhibited pleasure.

Her body was more ample and mature than was apparent under the male clothes she had been wearing. Her breasts were full and firm, with rosy nipples puckered and prominent from the chill of the underground water. Her waist was long and slender, her belly as flat and firm as the polished stone walls around her. When she turned with her back to him, he caught a glimpse of a pale rounded rear end that tapered delicately down to a pair of long, slender legs. She stood slightly bowlegged, as if from a lifelong familiarity with the back of a horse. As she appeared now, long hair down, letting the sheets of falling water ripple across her body, she seemed nothing like the tough-talking young hellion he had encountered such a short time before.

But despite the alluring vision she presented, reality was still not far away. Her Winchester rifle lay with her clothes on a large stone near the edge of the pool.

For a while Raider had nothing better to do than simply to lie there watching her splash about in the water. She washed her body down with a large cake of soap, rinsing frequently under the waterfall, then washed her long brown hair and rinsed again. Despite the desperate situation he was in, he could feel his body responding to the appealing sight of her. It was ridiculous, but not too surprising, he thought.

When her bath was finished, Lucy stepped out of the water and began toweling herself dry. It was then that she happened to glance in Raider's direction and noticed that he had been watching her. A frown crossed her face. "What are you staring at?" she asked.

"I'm having a look at your goods," Raider told her.

"Well, I hope you're enjoying yourself, 'cause mine are the last you'll ever see."

"Seems like," Raider admitted.

"Frank and Jesse are out scouting around right now," she said, "and if they find out there's no kind of law close by, you're finished. Jesse'll see to that." As she spoke, she was putting her pants and shirt on. When that was done, she sat down on the rock beside her rifle and pulled on her socks and calfskin boots.

"Who are you, Lucy?" Raider asked her. "What are you doing with these two, and where's the rest of their gang?"

"So many questions from a dead man! What does it matter to you now?"

"If I am a dead man, then what would it hurt to answer?"

"All right then," she decided, picking up her rifle and coming over near the fire. Raider rolled back over with some difficulty. "My name is Lucy Samuels, and I'm Frank and Jesse's cousin on their mama's side. I wished I rode in their gang, but they won't let me. Right now we're just traveling together, and we stopped off here for a few days."

"Well, where's the others, the Younger brothers, Charlie Pitts, Clel Miller, and all the rest?"

"I don't know," Lucy replied. "I haven't seen them on this trip. It's just been Frank and Jesse and me, all the ways from Texas."

"Texas?" Raider asked. "Is that where you've come from?"

"It's where I live," she said. "Me and my mama. But I'm traveling back east for a visit. We've been on the road for near a week now."

The information that Lucy was giving him confused Raider. The bank robbery in Kansas City was what? Four days ago? And now she was saying that they had been traveling from Texas for the past week and that she hadn't seen any of the other members of the gang during all that time. Either Lucy Samuels was more of a skilled liar than she appeared to be, or Doc's earlier suspicions had been right and the James Gang had not robbed the Fidelity National.

"Just tell me one more thing, Lucy," Raider said. "Where's Nellie? Nothing's happened to her, has it?"

"She's fine," Lucy assured him. "She was wore out, and I took her back in one of the little crannies where we sleep and let her use my pallet."

"I wasn't lying to your cousin when I told him she has nothing to do with the Pinkertons," he said. "She followed us here to Caseyville and she followed me into this cave, but it was just to get a story for her newspaper. I ain't all that anxious to catch a bullet myself, but it would really be a shame if she got hurt too. Nellie's been a pain in the ass to us, but she's no threat to the three of you."

"Since when does a lousy Pinkerton start worrying about innocent bystanders?" a male voice asked from the direction of the cave entrance. Raider looked around awkwardly in that direction and saw that Frank and Jesse had just come in.

"It's been a habit of me and my partner right along," Raider said.

"Well you sure as hell weren't worried about it when you crippled our mama and killed our little brother," Jesse sneered. "And me and Frank weren't even there that night they raided Mama's house."

"I can't deny it happened," Raider said. "But from all I heard, it was an accident. The word I got was the posse pitched a flare into the house and your stepfather kicked it into the fireplace. That's where it blew up."

"Well, it sure as hell won't be any accident when I drop

the hammer on you, Pink," Jesse said.

"But we don't intend to harm your young friend," Frank added. "The newspaper she works for, the Kansas City *Times*, has always been sympathetic to our cause, so we'll spare her life."

"Your cause?"

Frank James stared down at him for a moment, then said in a quiet, serious tone, "A long time ago it was a cause, and a damn good one, too. We rode proud and fought like devils for something we believed in with all our hearts."

"I can buy that much of what you say," Raider told him. "I'm from the South myself, and if the war had come along a few years later, I'd have probably been fighting for the same side you were. But later..."

"There never was no later for us," Jesse growled. "The damn Yankees never let the war end for the men that rode in Quantrill's Raiders. After Gettysburg we went home and tried to settle down, but they wouldn't let us. Our friends were getting jailed and lynched and blamed for every holdup for three hundred miles around, so finally we decided that it we were going to get blamed for them, we might as well be doing them."

It was a familiar story to Raider, though he had never heard it directly from any former Confederate guerrilla before. After each of the James Gang's major robberies, the newspapers sympathetic to the James brothers and their comrades always reprinted lengthy explanations of how the former rebels had been forced into outlawry by the policies and intolerance of the victorious North. Even though his sympathies naturally resided with the defeated Southern cause, the rationalizations never quite washed with Raider.

"Jesse and I both have wives and children now," Frank said. "We've spent most of the years since the war moving from one place to another, living under fake names, holed up half the time in places like this away from our families, always having to watch our backsides for men like you. Do you think we're content with the life we've been forced into?"

"I think there's a part of it you couldn't live without anymore," Raider told him honestly. "I mean the robbing and killing part."

"Shit, Frank. What are we standing here arguing with this jackass for? We've got to cover some miles before that other Pinkerton in town finds some way to put a posse together." He stepped forward, drew his revolver, and pointed it at Raider's head, all with a chilling sort of calm. "Believe me, Pink, this is going to be a real pleasure."

Raider stared up at the blue steel barrel and the cold eyes of the man who wielded it. He was determined to die as good as he could, and with a defiant word on his lips.

"Will it be as enjoyable as gunning down that unarmed old woman in Kansas City?" he asked. In the next instant he expected the gun to go off, but instead the hand that held it wavered slightly. Anger flared in Jesse's eyes.

"I've never killed a woman!" he snarled.

"Her name was Helen Finman, and she was probably about your mother's age," Raider said. He was no longer even sure that they were responsible for the robbery, and he was making up most of what he said. An old woman had been shot, but Raider knew nothing about her. But his ramblings seemed to be buying him additional seconds of life, so he continued. "She had three grandchildren, and she was taking some money out of the bank for presents."

"We didn't rob that goddamn bank!" Jesse hissed.

"It's the truth," Frank said. "We weren't the ones."

"Why explain that to a dead man?" Raider said.

"Somebody went to a lot of trouble to make it look like our work," Frank said. "But of all the jobs we've pulled, we've never killed just for the hell of it. That's not our way."

"And we've never killed women," Jesse insisted angrily. "That's why we're here, to find the ones that done it and settle up with them."

"What do you know about this thing, Pink?" Frank asked. Raider tried not to let his relief show as he watched the barrel of Jesse's revolver slowly drop. He still wasn't dead. Not quite.

"Most everybody is sure you did it," Raider said. "The only doubts I've heard came from my partner in town."

Lucy, who had been standing off to the side all this time, stepped forward at last and said, "We were over in Coffeeville when word came in about the holdup."

"That's right," Frank said. "And after that we stopped here because we wanted to know who would use our names to butcher people during a robbery. It was just late yesterday that I heard from a contact of ours up near Kansas City, and now we've got a line on the bastards we're after."

"Frank, just why in the hell are we explaining all this to him?" Jesse asked. The barrel of the pistol rose again, and Raider tensed.

"I'm not sure," Frank said. His eyes were intent on Raider. "Let me think about this thing a minute."

"Even if you didn't rob that bank, and even if you catch up with the ones who did," Raider suggested, "who's going to believe your side of things?"

"One thing's sure," Jesse said. "They won't be around to do it again."

"But he's right, Jesse," Frank told his brother. "It still won't clear our names. People will always wonder if maybe we don't gun down old ladies for no good cause."

"We'll just have to live with it," Jesse said.

"But not if we had some proof. Or not if we had somebody with us that the law would believe."

"No, Frank. Goddamn it, no!"

"How bad do you want to live, Pink?" Frank James asked Raider.

"As much as most any other man," Raider admitted. "But not under any circumstances."

"Damn it, Frank!" Jesse stormed. "No!"

Raider had only a vague notion of what the elder James

brother might have in mind, but if it contained the possibility of his survival, he thought it was sure worth listening to.

"Look, Jesse," Frank reasoned. "He may be a Pinkerton, but he didn't blow up our little brother any more than we robbed that bank in Kansas City. If he agreed to whatever terms we decided to lay down . . ."

"Trust a Pinkerton?" Jesse exclaimed. "Shit! I'm killing the bastard."

"Think about it, Jesse. Just take a second to think the whole thing through."

"Just what in the world are you two talking about?" Lucy asked at last. "I don't understand anything of what's going on."

"He thinks maybe we could take this Pink with us and use him as proof that we didn't rob that bank," Jesse told her. "Is that it, Frank?"

"That's about the size of it," Frank agreed.

"Which means trusting a lousy, stinking Pinkerton." Jesse spat on the cave floor.

"I don't expect there to be much trust on either side," Frank admitted. "But you remember, back during the war, we did strike a truce once in a while with the Yankees. When the reason was good enough, we made a truce, and usually it worked. I'm not so crazy about the notion of keeping him alive when it would be a hell of a lot easier just to kill him, but in this case . . ."

"It's the craziest damn thing I ever heard of in my life," Jesse grumbled. "Trusting a Pinkerton man." But despite his words, Raider thought he detected a barely perceptible change in the outlaw's tone. His determination to kill Raider seemed to be wavering.

"How about it, Pink?" Frank asked.

"A truce, huh?" Raider said. "Your brother's right. It is crazy, but still . . . The fact is, my partner and I are working on the bank robbery case. We're out to get the men who did it, no matter who they are. Another time we might be assigned to hunt the two of you, but that's not our orders right now." He paused a moment, gauging their reaction to his words, then added, "And by the way, the name's Raider."

Jesse holstered his pistol. "We've got to talk about this, Frank. By ourselves."

"All right," Frank said. "Lucy, you go wake that reporter and then get everything together. We'll be pulling out soon." He followed his brother out of the chamber.

Nellie Rosemond had just reached Raider and was kneeling at his side when the brothers returned.

"All right, here's the terms, Raider," Frank James said. "The truce lasts until we find the bastards that robbed the bank and nail their hides. We haven't worked everything out about giving you your gun back, but whether we do or not, you've got to agree not to try to use it on us or take us into custody. And you won't make any attempt to contact your people until we get the job done. Can you live with that?"

"As long as we're going after the bank robbers," Raider said.

"Raider, what in the world . . . ?" Nellie began.

"What about her?" Raider interrupted.

"She's going with us," Frank said. "At least partways."

Raider looked back at Nellie. "I'll tell you all about it later."

Jesse James nudged him in the back with his boot. "You listen to me, mister, and listen good."

Raider met his cold stare.

"From now till we get this thing settled, if you ever . . ." Jesse threatened.

"Or if *you* ever . . ." Raider challenged.

Raider decided that would pretty much be the tone of this unholy partnership.

Raider's arms and legs were stiff. He knew it would take days for the rope burns to heal on his wrists. But it was a relief to be free, and a definite pleasure to still be alive. A couple of times there, things had looked pretty grim. Later, if he tried to tell this story, he wondered how many people would believe he had looked down the bore of Jesse James's revolver and lived to tell about it.

From somewhere, Frank had acquired two additional horses for Raider and Nellie to ride. They were adequate mounts, but nowhere near the magnificent animals that Frank, Jesse, and Lucy rode. The outlaws also seemed well equipped and supplied, and within thirty minutes of Raider's release from bondage, they were ready to strike out. Neither of the brothers had yet told him where they were going, but he assumed he would be told more as their confidence in him increased. Right now they were still watching him closely, and the holster slapping against his side remained empty.

One of the main problems Raider grappled with was the matter of Doc. What Allan Pinkerton and the others might or might not think about his disappearance was of no major concern to him, but he was worried about the conclusions Doc might make.

Whenever Doc came out to the cave, as he inevitably would when Raider did not return, what he would find there was certain to cause him alarm. Evidence that somebody had been staying in Clemmens Cavern was abundant, but there would be no trace of anything left behind to indicate what had happened to Raider. The logical conclusions Doc could draw were that his partner had either been captured by the cave's occupants or lost somewhere within the mountain's hollow innards.

But there was nothing Raider could do about it. Trying to leave any sort of message or sign behind for Doc would be a violation of the agreement he had made with the outlaws, and if it was discovered it would surely mean instant death for him. When it was all over, Raider decided, he could contact his partner immediately and let him know the unusual terms of the pact he had made for the sake of their assignment and, in fact, to save his own life.

Frank, Raider, and the two women were gathered just outside the entrance to the cave, their horses saddled and ready. Jesse had ridden out a few minutes before to scout the surrounding area, and they were waiting for him to return so they could leave.

"I guess we'll have to scratch Clemmens Cavern off our list of safe hideouts now," Frank commented.

"Too bad," Raider drawled.

"It really is," Frank said, taking no offense at Raider's minor sarcasm. "Used to be, this was one of our best. It's got two back ways out, and one of them's good enough to lead horses through. I don't think anybody in this area knows about that one, except maybe a few of the old-timers."

"You mean . . . ?" Raider said, turning to glare at Frank James.

"I didn't want to make it too easy for you." Frank chuckled.

"Shit!" Raider grumbled.

"Another thing we've always liked about this place was the people," the outlaw noted. "Back during the war a Yankee outfit got it in their heads that they were going to burn Caseyville to the ground. Quantrill got wind of it, and he sent some of us down here to put a stop to it. We rode all night to get here. We covered sixty-two miles in nine hours, and we reached the Yankees at dawn, while they were still in bivouac. Only three of them survived, and two of those decided to join up with us. People in little towns like Caseyville remember things like that for a long time."

"They sure weren't falling all over each other to help me and Doc," Raider agreed.

"They knew we were here. Everybody knew we were here, and they knew who you two were, too."

"Yeah," Raider said. "That business about the railroad passes isn't a mistake Doc and I are likely to make twice."

Their conversation was interrupted by the sound of a horse galloping along the narrow trail that snaked along the mountainside toward the cave entrance. Frank James drew his revolver and waited until his brother came into view before reholstering it.

"Things look fine," Jesse announced. "I didn't see nothing moving on the trail but snakes and rabbits."

"All right then, let's get going," Frank said, stepping up into the saddle.

"NOT JUST YET, GENTLEMEN!"

The voice came from the rocks above the cave entrance, and Raider knew who he would see there even before he had a chance to glance up. Doc was lying atop a rocky outcropping directly above the mouth of the cavern, pointing Raider's carbine down at the two brothers. He was no more than thirty feet away, and from the position he was in, he had both the outlaws cold.

"If either one of you even tries to sneeze, I'll blast you out of the saddle," Doc announced. "Get their guns, Raider."

Raider hesitated and looked up toward his partner. "Uh... Listen, Doc..."

"For heaven's sake, get their guns," Doc repeated.

"Look, maybe you'd better hand them over," Raider suggested to the two outlaws.

"Like hell I will, you—" Jesse snarled. He was interrupted by a shot that gnawed a neat plug of leather out of the saddle horn between his knees.

Doc quickly jacked another shell in the chamber before either of the brothers had time to draw. "You get the next one in the side of your head," he warned.

Raider took the handguns from Frank and Jesse's holsters, then covered them while Doc scrambled down from his rocky perch.

"I knew something had gone wrong," Doc said as he joined his partner. "When you didn't come back all night, I went ahead and sent the wire out, but I knew I couldn't wait for everybody else to get here. It looks like I got here just in time, too. I've been up there in the rocks for about ten minutes. I was just waiting for the second one to get back."

"Doc, I've got to tell you something..." Raider began.

"It's them, isn't it, partner? We've captured Frank and Jesse James."

"That's what I need to talk to you about. You see..."

"The last I heard, the reward was up to ten thousand apiece for these two. And besides that, we'll be able to write our own ticket with the old man. By God, we did it!" Doc was busting his buttons with excitement.

"Goddamn it, will you shut up a minute!" Raider stormed.

The look of surprise on Doc's face changed to confusion and alarm when he noticed that his partner was no longer even making a pretense of keeping his guns trained on the outlaws.

"These two are the James brothers all right, Doc," Raider said, trying to discover a good starting point. "But we haven't exactly got them captured."

CHAPTER EIGHT

The road wound its way up the steep hillside in a series of reptilian switchbacks. The rocky slope was populated with outcroppings of trees and brush that clung tenaciously to their toeholds in the sandy soil. The roadbed itself was a nightmare of ruts, washed-out stretches, and perilous cliffs over which man and animal might plunge hundreds of feet straight down at the slightest misstep. Far behind them, the valley they had just left and the town of Caseyville were laid out below like a scenic panorama. The road led west toward Kansas.

On Doc's signal, Raider dropped back and attempted to ride beside the wagon. But in many places the roadbed was simply too narrow to permit such a thing, so instead Raider tied his mount to the back of the wagon and climbed up on the seat beside Doc.

"This is hell," Doc admitted, staring at the way ahead with open dread.

"Well, you insisted on going back for Judith and the wagon," Raider reminded him. "You were warned."

"I didn't think it would be *this* bad," Doc said. "One little slip and..." His eyes wandered out over the sheer drop-off at the edge of the road to complete the statement. "And besides, I wanted to see if I'd gotten any response to that telegram I sent."

"And you found out."

"Sure, I found out that the operator never even sent it. On Frank James's instructions."

"The people in these parts feel obligated to them from way back during the war."

"Yeah," Doc complained. "I've gotten the impression that if the James brothers asked the people of Caseyville to sacrifice a virgin, they'd gladly haul out the parson's daughter and start a bonfire."

"The war was a big deal in these parts," Raider said. "It was uglier here than in a lot of other places."

They rode on in silence for a couple of minutes, each thinking his own thoughts. Raider felt good having his heavy Remington .44 back in his holster where it belonged. That was one of the amendments to the agreement after Doc got the drop on the two outlaws. Now everybody went armed.

"Tell me something, Rade," Doc said at last, speaking in a quiet, almost reflective tone of voice. "Has it fully soaked into your head that we're traveling in the company of the two most wanted bank and train robbers in the United States? Have you considered all the implications of what that means?"

"I'll admit, a man might tend to let a couple of implications slip past him when he's got somebody pointing a gun at his head ready to pull the trigger," Raider drawled sarcastically. "But it did seem like a good bargain at the time I made it, and it still does. Besides, I gave my word. We're committed."

"I know," his partner said regretfully. "But I'm still bothered by the moral implications of this thing. Aren't we supposed to be on the side of the law?"

"I musta left my badge pinned to my other shirt," Raider said.

"You know what I mean, Rade."

"We're detectives, Doc. Pinkerton operatives. And our job right now is to catch up with nine sonsabitches that robbed a bank and killed a bunch of folks. That's as far as I've taken the thing in my head. If you want to wrestle around with a bunch of moral implications or some bullshit like that, just leave me out of it."

"It's not likely to stop bothering me," Doc admitted. "But you are right about one thing. We're committed."

"Committed as hell," Raider agreed. "But only to the point when we catch up to the bank robbers. Then all bets are off."

"That's another thing that's got me worried," Doc said. "When it's all over, we'll still be Pinkertons, and the James brothers are none too fond of our kind."

"But they won't do anything about it, because they'll still need us. That's the only reason we're along on this picnic, to spread the word that it wasn't the James Gang that held up that bank. If it wasn't for that, my corpse would already be sprouting moss back there in Clemmens Cavern."

"It's strange to think two outlaws would be so concerned over their reputation, though. There's no telling how many men those two up there have killed in their lifetimes. Dozens, I'd say."

"Sure, but where would it put them if word spread that they'd taken to killing old women and innocent bystanders just for the hell of it? I'd say they wouldn't be none too welcome even in places like Caseyville no more."

"It would damage the cavalier reputations that they've been so careful to construct over the years," Doc said. "But damnation, Raider! To find ourselves cooperating with Frank and Jesse James..."

"Uh huh."

When the road crested the mountainside, they could tell that the ascent on the far side would be a little less treacherous. In the distance the hills began to rise less prominently and the countryside promised easier travel. Raider returned to horseback and moved ahead to catch up with Frank James, who was riding point.

"Are you ready to talk about where we're going yet?" Raider asked. The tone of things had changed considerably after the incident back at the mouth of the cavern. The brothers had been amazed when Raider talked his partner out of taking them back as prisoners, and after that their trust in him had risen considerably.

"To tell you the truth," Frank said, "I'm not exactly sure. While we were holed up there in Caseyville, I got word from a friend that there's some new talent going to work in this area. Nobody knows for sure yet who they are, but they're operating from somewhere in southeastern Kansas. Jesse and I think they might be the ones who took the bank in Kansas City. For now, all we plan to do is visit a few towns and keep our eyes and ears open."

"It's a slim lead to go on," Raider complained. "I thought you had something better than that. At least some names or something."

"Do you think it would have made a difference back there in the cave if you'd known the truth?"

"I wasn't in such a good bargaining position at the time. It's damned hard to argue with the business end of a .45."

"Especially Jesse's .45," Frank said.

"That's the damned truth," Raider agreed.

They camped in the wilds the first night. Midway into the second day they passed into the flat, arid countryside of southeastern Kansas. There were few travelers on the road they were using, and no one they encountered seemed interested in the party of four men and two women riding peacefully westward. They skirted the first few small settlements they encountered, mainly on the insistence of the James brothers.

The two outlaws became noticeably more nervous once they had left the Missouri border behind, and a couple of times Jesse made ambiguous comments about crossing over into "enemy territory."

The rivalries and hatreds between the residents of the two states dated back to the 1850s, when raids back and forth between the freestaters of Kansas Territory and the pro-slavery populace of Missouri were common. The bitterness only intensified with the advent of the war and the admission of Kansas into the Union as a free state. Frank James had taken part in William Quantrill's famous and devastating raid on Lawrence, Kansas, in 1863.

Now, considerably more than a decade after the war, the brothers still realized how much danger they would face if their presence was detected in Kansas. Unlike their home state of Missouri, they could count on little or no support from the people of the Kansas countryside. Frank explained to Doc and Raider that during their infrequent incursions into the state, the brothers used the names B. J. Woodson and Thomas Howard.

Near dusk of the second evening, they stopped at a cottonwood grove on the banks of one of the rare streams in the area. While the others began unloading their gear and making camp, Doc borrowed Raider's horse and rode off to secure permission to stay there from the residents of a ramshackle farm a short distance away.

The squat log house was about fifteen feet wide and twice as long. Waist-high prairie grasses grew on the sod roof of the building, and the fences and outbuildings that surrounded it appeared to be as badly in need of repair as the main house. Half a dozen ragged horses stood in a corral behind the house, languidly munching hay, and a few head of cattle dotted the open range nearby. The place could easily have been deserted, except for the livestock and a thin ribbon of smoke that rose lazily from a low stone chimney.

Doc paused his horse several yards from the front door and called out, "Hello the house!"

A couple of shadowy faces peered out through the two small windows in front, then the front door opened a crack. A rifle barrel emerged, followed by a shuffling man.

"Evening," Doc offered amiably.

"'Pears to be," the man replied. He wore a scraggly beard that seemed to be more the result of neglect than a desire to be bearded. It was difficult to judge his age beneath the filth and the floppy felt hat he wore, but Doc would have guessed him to be nearly sixty. He wore a faded longjohn shirt beneath his frayed bib overalls, and his feet were bare. Behind him a couple of male faces peered out through the open door from the dusky interior of the house, and two or three more stared at him from the windows. All of them struck Doc as vaguely moronic.

"My name is Dr. Weatherbee, and I'm traveling through your area with a party of acquaintances," Doc announced.

"We ain't got nothin' you can have," the man said, advancing a few feet into the open area in front of the door and tilting the muzzle of his rifle down at last. "No vittles nor feed for your stock, so don't go askin'." A figure eased out the front door of the house, then another and another. All appeared to be in their twenties, and each of them resembled the older man in some way. Undoubtedly they were his sons, as were the two others who remained inside the house. Doc saw no signs of any female presence around the place.

"We don't need anything from you," Doc explained.

"But we planned to camp by that little stream just south of here, and I wanted to get your permission in case we're on your land."

The old man tilted his head to the side, as if that might be a better angle from which to study Doc. In a way Doc could not quite understand, the appraisal seemed to have a threatening undertone. In a moment Doc's glance shifted to the younger men. One of them had a pistol stuck down into the waistband of his trousers, and another wore a large knife in a sheath on his belt. All were as filthy and somber as their sire.

"It's my land," the old man confirmed. "What's it worth to you to stay there?"

"Nothing," Doc replied. "We'll simply move on if that's what you decide."

"Let 'em stay, Pa," one of the younger men suggested.

"Shut yer yap, Hiram," the father snapped. "It's me that's doin' the hagglin' here."

"There's nothing to haggle over, sir," Doc told him. "Either you let us stay or you don't. But we won't do any damage to your property, and we'll be gone by first light tomorrow."

The younger man stepped up to his father and spoke to him in a tone too low for Doc to hear. They talked briefly, then the old man turned back to Doc and asked, "How many be you?"

"Four men and two women."

They talked again, then the old man said, "A'right, you kin stay." Beside him, his son was grinning like a cat with a mouthful of canary, an expression Doc did not find particularly comforting.

"I thank you, Mr. . . . ?"

"Binder, Noah Binder," the man said. "But don't let us catch you tryin' to steal nothin' after dark," he warned. "If you do, you get this." He raised the rifle and pointed it at Doc again.

After a quick glance around the place, Doc wondered what in creation the old man might believe was valuable enough to steal. Even the livestock hardly appeared to be worth the effort.

"Your property is safe, Mr. Binder," Doc assured him. Feeling rather uncomfortable, Doc turned his horse and rode away. After he had crossed nearly half of the quarter mile to the stream, he glanced back and saw that Binder and his sons were standing just as they had been, staring after him.

The camp was just out of sight of the house over a slight hummock. By the time Doc reached it, Raider had built a fire and the two women were at work preparing a meal of salt meat and tinned beans. Both Jesse and Frank had withdrawn a short distance away, keeping their own company. They were sitting on the bank of the stream, cleaning their weapons.

"Are we clear to stay?" Raider asked Doc as he stepped out of the saddle.

"I guess we are," Doc said. "But those are some strange people over there. Very strange."

"Folks get to acting curious when they live out by themselves like this," Raider said, dismissing his partner's apprehensions. "You're just not used to their kind."

"Maybe that's all it is," Doc replied as he turned to unsaddle the horse. But he wasn't sure. He knew strangeness when he saw it, and Noah Binder and his several sons were definitely a strange lot.

CHAPTER NINE

By the time they finished their evening meal, full darkness had arrived and the moon was just rising. While they were all eating, Nellie Rosemond had tried briefly to draw the James brothers into a conversation about their lives of crime but both became tight-lipped and guarded when banks and trains became the topic of talk.

Later Doc took Nellie off to show her the collection of photographic equipment in the back of his wagon, and Raider decided to take a stroll along the bank of the stream to settle his supper. As the light of the campfire faded behind him, he heard light footsteps tracing his path and paused to let Lucy Samuels catch up with him.

"What's this?" he asked her. "Did your cousins send you along to keep an eye on me?"

"No," she told him defensively, but after a couple of more steps she admitted, "Well, maybe Frank did say something of the sort. But you know how careful we got to be."

"As a matter of fact," Raider drawled, "what I had in mind was to sneak back around to the edge of camp and blast both of them from behind. And you, too. I thought it would be a lot more fun than killing the lot of you back there in Caseyville when I had the chance. That's the way us lousy Pinkertons are."

"You sure got a smart mouth, mister," Lucy snapped.

"Yup."

A hostile silence hung between them as they reached the edge of the grove and dropped down into the streambed. The water was low at this time of year, and a soft carpet of grass covered much of the ground beneath their feet. On either side, the banks rose higher than their heads, indicating the volume of water that the stream must carry during the spring runoffs.

"It wouldn't take so much effort just to be civil," Lucy offered at last. "Do you have some kind of big problem with that?"

"Not particularly."

"Well then, what is eating at you?"

"It's you," Raider said. "It's you being with those two and thinking they're such fine examples of what a man oughta be."

"They're my kin," Lucy said.

"But that don't make everything they do right," Raider argued. "They rob banks and trains, for chrissake! They steal other people's money at the point of a gun, and they don't bat an eye at having to kill anybody that tries to get in their way. For the life of me, I can't figure where the glory is in shit like that."

"I understand why they're the way they are," she told him. "After the war was over, the Yankees—"

"What a goddamn load of crap!" Raider interrupted. "I

never met a crook yet who had the grit to admit he stole things just because he was dishonest or because he was too goddamn lazy to work for his money and live within the law. They always gotta come up with some kind of bullshit excuses why they *have* to live like they do.

"Tell me something, little girl. If they was to let you ride with them and you took up the outlaw life, what would *your* excuse be? The first time you had to put a bullet between the shoulder blades of a four-eyed little bank clerk that panicked and ran for the door, what would you tell yourself so that it would feel all right inside what you did?"

Lucy was quiet for a few seconds, but finally she replied with hesitant defiance, "I guess I don't know about all that, since I ain't no big-shot Pinkerton detective. But I can tell you one thing. I'm no little girl."

"I seen," Raider reminded her. He let a slight smile ease the tension of the moment. He wasn't going to change the course of her life in the space of a few minutes, so what was the use of arguing?

"You're not the first," Lucy told him. "I'm no hussy, but I am a woman inside and out."

"I'm sure you are."

"Do you want to know how I felt when you were looking at me in that cave?" She paused, embarrassed by the subject she found herself discussing, but compelled to go on.

"How?" Raider prompted her.

"Like I didn't want to put my clothes on just yet," she admitted. "It was crazy. There you were, a damned Pinkerton, trussed up like a calf for branding and waiting for Jesse's bullet to end it for you, but I still felt things stirring around inside of me."

"That was crazy," Raider confirmed. "But you know what? I felt a few cravings of my own." He stopped and looked down at her in the moonlight, then added, "Just like now."

"So you think it ain't fitting for a girl to be out robbing

banks," Lucy said with an impish grin, "but it's a whole different matter for her to share her personals with strangers?"

"Most times the last don't seem to harm nobody."

"That might be the first thing we've agreed on all night," Lucy said softly.

Her breath quickened as soon as Raider took her in his arms. Her lips were moist and warm, and after a moment she began to return his kisses hungrily. He fumbled impatiently with the buttons on the front of her shirt, opening them far enough to reach inside and swallow one of her breasts in his hand.

"God, your hands are rough," she said. Raider couldn't tell whether that fact irritated or stimulated her, but by the way her nipple probed at his palm, he assumed it was the latter. He caught the rising projection of flesh between his fingers and caressed it, eliciting a sigh from Lucy.

"My cousins would shoot you dead if they caught you out here groping me," Lucy warned.

"It's more fun when there's a risk."

Lucy started having second thoughts when she realized how far and how fast Raider intended to go. He had her blouse open before she hardly knew it, and what had only moments before been a fanciful conversation about sex was quickly becoming the act itself.

"Look, Raider," she told him between passionate kisses. "I'm not sure we should just . . ." Her resistance was weak, and when he leaned down and closed his mouth over one nipple, it ended completely. She closed her eyes and tilted her head back, sucking in the cool night air. "Oh my god."

Their clothing seemed to melt from their bodies, though it was actually all Raider's doing. His hands roamed her hot flesh at their leisure, spreading pleasure wherever they wandered and heightening the wanton abandon that was quickly taking control of both of them. Lucy writhed in his arms like a wild creature, hungry for release, but not freedom.

He laid her down on the soft grass of the creek bed and descended on top of her. She shivered and said, "Damn, that's cold on a girl's bare backside."

"You'll forget about it in a second," he promised. He plunged his erect cock straight into her, guided unerringly to that precious spot as if by primal instinct. Her quim was tight, but quickly accommodated him with a surge of hot female juices. Her back arched up, flattening her full breasts between their chests. Raider's tongue plunged into her mouth, emulating the act that their bodies were performing farther below.

"Easy, Raider. Easy!" Lucy pleaded as his hips arched and descended, ramming his cock home with telling force. But it was too late for prolonged refinements. His blood was rushing, his lust was nearing a frenzied peak, and the urge to come was practically overwhelming.

"Oh, damn, that...hurts...good," she sighed. He knew that the weight of his body must be crushing her smaller frame and that his stabs into her flesh were probably causing her as much pain as pleasure, but... Her cunt grabbed at him suddenly, and the prolonged moan that came from deep within her reverberated off the dirt walls on either side of them. Her pelvis bucked up insistently, her sex still clutching at his swollen penis, and Raider snorted like an angry bull. His semen pulsed into her as his cock became the focus of all that was important to him in the world at the moment. The sensation surged nearly to the point of becoming unbearable, then slowly began to subside.

Lucy was gasping for air beneath him. Raider rose weakly onto his hands and knees. His erection wilted as it slipped out of her and met the cool night air.

"Not bad for a little country girl, huh?" Lucy asked.

"Tolerable," Raider said, grinning down at her. He moved to the side carefully and sat cross-legged on the ground next to her. Her slender body seemed to glow in the soft moonlight, relaxed, fulfilled, and youthfully alive. Her hand strayed down and idly stroked the lips of her cunt, as if in remembrance of the recent visitor there.

"They'll probably kick you out of the clan if they ever learn you up and did it with a Pinkerton man." Raider chuckled.

"It wouldn't be out of the question," Lucy agreed with a smile. "I was thirteen years old before I learned that you could say the word 'Pinkerton' without having to put the word 'damn' in front of it." She closed her eyes, relaxing with the feeling of Raider's light touch on her breasts and belly. Then she looked over at him and said, "But this really doesn't change a thing, does it?"

"What do you mean?" Raider asked.

"This that we did here, it doesn't change how it is between your people and mine, does it?"

"Not likely," Raider replied. "But then, it wasn't meant to. It was just—"

"Just fucking?" Suddenly her tone was chilly, and Raider couldn't understand why.

"That's what it boils down to, I guess," he admitted. "But what else did you expect it to mean? What did you expect from me?"

"Nothing," Lucy snapped, sitting up suddenly and reaching for her clothes. "I didn't expect anything from that or from you."

They dressed under a cloud of unexplainable hostility. Raider let his mind worry over the subject for a while longer, then finally dismissed it from his thoughts under the general category of "women." That automatically labeled it as a matter he might as well resign himself to never understanding completely.

But on the way back to camp Lucy softened up a little. She took his hand as they walked and softly told him, "It's not your fault, Raider."

"What isn't?" he asked.

"I mean how I feel isn't your fault," she said, wrestling

with her emotions and trying to explain them. "It's all so confusing for me. Two days ago in that cave you were such a terrible fellow in my eyes. A damn Pinkerton! I was fully prepared to stand by and watch my cousin Jesse put a bullet in you because you were such a terrible enemy. And then tonight, there we were, going at it like crazy. And it was so doggoned good. I guess that's what bothers me as much as anything else. Pinkerton or not, enemy or not, I loved it, and somewhere inside there was this feeling that I wasn't supposed to."

"You're thinking about it too much, girl," Raider said lightly. "That'll give you problems every time."

They were nearing the place where they had descended into the creek bed earlier. The bank sloped at a less forbidding angle there, and it would be no problem to climb back out. But just before they started up, Raider froze and gave Lucy's hand a firm squeeze. She knew what the signal meant and stopped instantly at his side.

They remained like that for a moment, attuning their senses to the nighttime around them. Then Raider leaned his head down close to hers and whispered, "I heard something up there. About where the trees start." Lucy stared at him in alarm but said nothing.

"You wait here a minute," Raider instructed her. "I'm going to have a look around. It might have just been a rabbit or a steer, but I'd better make sure."

Lucy hunched down against the creek bank while Raider moved forward another few yards, then eased slowly up the side. He stopped when he was able to peer over the rim of the bank and into the cottonwood grove. After two or three minutes, he retraced his steps and knelt down beside her.

"I saw at least two people just into the edge of the trees," he whispered. "I bet they're from that farmhouse over there. Doc told me earlier he didn't like the looks of those folks."

"But what would they want from us?" Lucy asked.

"Anything they can get, I expect. Since they only saw

Doc, they might have us pegged for a bunch of dudes that can't handle ourselves in a scrap."

"I wonder how they'd feel if they knew who they were really slipping up on?" Lucy speculated. Despite the crisis, there was a trace of pride in her voice.

"We need to ease on down the stream and see if we can't get to the camp and warn the others."

"Why not just open up on them?" Lucy suggested. "That would be warning enough."

"Could be they're just nosy and don't mean us any harm," Raider said. "There's no use in killing anybody that doesn't need killing. It would be better to pass through this country without any trouble, if we can manage it."

Staying against the bank and moving as quietly as they could, they started west toward the camp. Raider guessed that the camp was about fifty yards ahead, and the flat land above would be lined with trees the whole way. They had covered about half the distance to the others when Raider halted again. This time Lucy immediately understood why. There was a rustle in the brush above them, and they heard the murmur of voices.

"Is that you, Hiram?" The voice was youthful and hesitant with fear.

"Damn it, Bo. Hush up! They'll hear you!" a more mature voice hissed. The brush rustled again, and the two seemed to meet on the bank directly above where Raider and Lucy were. If he leaned out a couple of feet, Raider believed he could have caught sight of them.

"I'm scared, Hiram," Bo whined. "Why do we have to do this, anyway?"

"You seen that feller, little brother," Hiram explained. "I bet his pockets was stuffed with greenbacks, and that horse he was on was better'n any I ever been astraddle. An' remember, he said they got wimmen with 'em. You figger you'll know what to do when your turn comes up with one of their wimmenfolk, Bo?"

"You think I'll hafta, Hiram?" the youth asked. "You reckon Pa's gonna make me?"

The old brother chuckled knowingly, then told him, "Shucks, it's as easy as falling down. It'll make a man out of you."

"I ain't so sure, Hiram."

"Just hush up and come on, Bo," Hiram ordered. "Likely Pa's in place now, an' we need to ease on up so we'll be ready."

When they had moved on away, Raider whispered to Lucy, "You stay put here while I go after those two. And don't try anything stupid. You heard what they were talking about, so after the fight's over, you'd best figure out who won before you come out in the open." Lucy nodded her agreement, and Raider slipped up the bank into the edge of the trees.

Raider hoped to capture the two brothers ahead of him without having to shoot them, which meant getting close enough to get the drop on them before sounding the alarm. It was risky, but there was no use in a lot of people getting killed unnecessarily. Keeping the two shadowy figures in sight most of the time, he tried to gain ground on them without making enough noise to give himself away. After a couple of minutes, he realized that he wasn't going to make it before they reached their position at the edge of the camp. He considered the problem for only an instant before coming to a decision.

Snapping off a quick shot in the air, he shouted, "Doc! It's an ambush." Then he went charging through the woods, directly at the pair he was following. Both the brothers spun in alarm to face him. The older of the two reacted with surprising speed. He raised his rifle to his shoulder and triggered a bullet singing past Raider's ear. Raider shot him in the center of his chest without even slowing down.

Things would have been fine. He could have reached the second brother and knocked him to the ground before the youth had time to use the enormous shotgun he was carrying. But a treacherous root reached up and grabbed the toe of Raider's boot, sprawling him to the ground within ten feet of the boy.

"Don't do it," he warned loudly as Bo raised the shotgun clumsily to his shoulder.

Fear and fury mingled on the boy's face. "You kilt Hiram!" he shrilled.

"Damn it, kid," Raider roared. "Don't!"

The youth had some difficulty thumbing the hammers back, but finally managed to get them cocked. Raider didn't bother to aim. There wasn't time, and at these close quarters there was no need. His shot ricocheted off the stock of the shotgun and entered the boy's chin from the underside. Both barrels of the shotgun discharged, but the youth was already falling backward at the time and the pellets tore harmlessly through a low-hanging branch above Raider's head.

In the back of his wagon, Doc had just claimed his first kiss from Nellie Rosemond when they heard the first shot and the shout from the woods. Neither of them was sure what was said, but the several shots that followed a moment later made the situation abundantly clear.

"Stay here," Doc said, shoving Nellie flat on the floor of the wagon and extinguishing the small kerosene lamp. By the time he retrieved his Diamondback .38 and a box of cartridges from a shelf, shots were already being fired from the woods nearby. Frank and Jesse were returning fire.

A bullet tore a chunk from the wagon door as Doc burst into the open, and others whined past him as he raced for the cover of a fallen log twenty feet away. He snapped off a couple of shots as he ran, then made a dive for the scant safety of the downed tree.

They were in an extremely vulnerable position, Doc realized. Their campfire clearly illuminated the clearing of their camp, and their attackers had the advantages of both the woods and the darkness. Risking a quick look, he saw that Frank was scantily concealed behind a couple of saddles he had piled together, and Jesse seemed to have made it to the haven of the bank of the stream. Both were firing with their rifles into the trees nearby.

Doc fired a couple of rounds at a muzzle flash in the trees, then ducked his head down just as a shotgun blast tore into the log.

"Micah, you an' Jonah circle to the right," a man called out in the darkness. Doc recognized Noah Binder's voice. He raised up and fired again, and somebody yelped somewhere back in the trees.

"Pa!" a young man called out in terror. "I'm shot, Pa! Help me!"

"In a minute, boy," Binder told him.

Doc lay flat on his back, hastily reloading the Diamondback. He knew he had to move and that he'd better do it fast. As soon as they circled, he would no longer be safe where he was. But which direction could he go? If he went to the right, he would cross Frank and Jesse's line of fire, but going to the left would draw fire on the wagon where Nellie was. That left only one option.

He cut loose with a yell as he leaped to his feet. The Diamondback barked again and again as he raced forward into the trees, straight at the bushwhackers. A bullet tugged at the sleeve of his jacket and another kicked up a chunk of sod at his feet, but somehow he managed to make it to the haven of a huge cottonwood. There he paused for an instant to reload. Then he moved on.

The first of the Binders he came to was a young man of about twenty. He lay flat on his back on the ground, the left side of his shirtfront soggy with blood. Barely conscious, he raised his pistol with both hands and tried to aim. Doc's first shot caught him at the base of the neck. The second entered his skull just under his nose, obliterating his face in a splash of blood.

"Damn you all to hell!" Doc heard Noah Binder roar just to his right. "You kilt my boy!"

Doc dove for cover just as Binder's rifle went off. He rolled onto his side and brought the .38 up with his right hand. Binder fired again, but fury and grief were ruining his aim. The shot plowed into the ground a good two feet from its intended target.

Doc's shot caught Binder in the left shoulder and spun him back, but he didn't go down.

"My boy!" Binder squawled out. His movements were clumsy as he raised his rifle and pointed it once again in Doc's direction. Doc shot him twice in the belly, staggering him backwards another few feet. Still the mortally wounded man managed to hang onto his balance. And his weapon. Again the muzzle of Binder's rifle started to rise.

"Die, damn it," Doc roared. He took the time to aim carefully and shot Binder in the center of his chest. The rifle slipped out of Noah Binder's grasp and he fell back at last, dead before his body hit the ground.

Suddenly the woods were quiet. After all the chaos and shouting of a moment before, the silence was ominous. Doc remained where he was, letting his tension drain away and searching the shadows around him for further enemies. But nothing moved on any side.

There was a crashing through the brush a few dozen feet away on the right. The noise drew away from him slowly, but Doc wasn't in the mood to pursue. Finally he rose and started back the way he had come.

"It's me. Doc," he announced as he neared the camp.

Nellie Rosemond was just gathering her courage to peek out the back of the wagon as Doc neared. Across the clearing Frank James was sitting on the ground, examining a flesh wound on his left forearm. None of the others were anywhere in sight.

"Are you all right?" Doc asked Nellie as she climbed out of the wagon. She fell against him, trembling slightly and near tears.

"I'm fine," she said. "Just scared."

Still with his arm around Nellie, Doc turned and walked over to Frank. "It was the old man from the farmhouse and his boys," Doc said.

"I figured that," Frank said.

"Where's your brother?"

Before the elder James brother could answer, a single rifle shot sounded from far away in the direction of the farmhouse, followed by two more in quick succession. Frank just nodded his head in the direction of the shooting.

Soon Raider and Lucy came easing cautiously into the edge of the clearing. When she saw her cousin's wound she hurried to help him.

Raider came over to Doc and Nellie. "I guess I'll listen closer the next time you tell me there's something strange about somebody," Raider admitted.

"It might have been pretty grim for us if you hadn't given us that warning," Doc said. "I got the old man and one of his boys. I haven't looked around for any more bodies."

"I had to take care of a couple of them," Raider said. "One wasn't hardly more than a boy, but he was armed like a man. He didn't even want to be out here, but he still had to die for his old man's greed."

Raider took a quick trip through the woods surrounding the camp, but found no more dead or wounded Binders. Just as he returned to the clearing from one side, Jesse entered from the other. He dropped tiredly to the ground beside his brother. Lucy was almost finished cleaning and dressing the wound on Frank's arm.

"So what happened out there?" Doc asked Jesse.

Jesse James glanced up, and the firelight danced in his dark, expressionless eyes. "We couldn't afford to leave any of them around to talk about this," he explained coldly. "I did what had to be done."

CHAPTER TEN

Nellie lay across the bed in Doc's hotel room, sighing with delight as Doc's fingers manipulated the tense muscles at the base of her neck.

"I could do a better job if you didn't have all these clothes in the way," he told her.

"Come on, Doc," Nellie giggled lightly. "If I was you and I couldn't come up with a better line than that, I think I'd give up trying to lure young women into my room to seduce them."

"You should consider yourself fortunate," Doc told her. "There's no telling what you might have to pay for a massage of this sort from a professional of my caliber."

"I know what price you'd have me pay." Nellie sighed.

She winced as Doc's knowing fingers began working their way down along her spine, kneading at knots of tension along the way.

This was the first time Doc had seen Nellie properly dressed and groomed since they'd left Caseyville a week before. The days on the road had been arduous for all of them, and by the time a halt was called at the end of each day's travel, there was little energy left for anything but the routine chores of making camp and preparing an evening meal. But finally they had decided to stop for a couple of days here in Dulcinda to get some proper rest.

"I wonder what the others are up to right now?" Nellie said.

"We're supposed to hear from them today," Doc said. "Frank has already been by the telegraph office once today, and I'm going to go after supper and check again."

"I hope they're all right," Nellie said. "It seems like a long time since we heard from them."

"It's only been two days," Doc told her.

After the annihilation of the Binder clan, life had become more complicated for the members of the group. They had been careful to conceal as much of the evidence as possible, placing all the bodies in Binder's ramshackle house and burning the place to the ground, but they knew eventually somebody was likely to go nosing around the farm and piece together some of what had happened. Frank James had been the first one to suggest that they split the party up, and for a while everybody else was opposed to the idea, including his brother. But when the outlaw had explained that a group their size tended to be conspicuous, and that if they all remained together they would be much easier to trace, Doc saw the logic of the suggestion. Eventually the others came around too.

Deciding who would go with whom was a thorny problem, but finally it was decided that Doc, Nellie, and Frank James would make up one group, while Raider, Lucy Samuels, and Jesse would comprise the other. Moving by horse-back, Raider's group would make a sweep north, stopping off in the towns along the way to ask a few discreet questions. Doc's party pushed straight west, performing the same duties. They made arrangements for keeping in occasional contact by telegraph, and both groups would eventually meet again at Wichita, in the south-central part of the state.

The new arrangements were hardly to anybody's liking, but considering the carnage they had been forced to commit on the Binder farm, it all seemed necessary.

When Doc's hands reached the small of Nellie's back, he pulled the tail of her blouse loose from the waistband of her skirt and ran his hands up under it. She wore a light silk camisole under the blouse, but at least it was a step in the right direction.

"Where's Frank now?" Nellie asked.

"He's asking around in the saloons," Doc said. "It's the best place to hear talk about owlhoots and holdups if there's any going around."

"Isn't that dangerous for him?"

"Probably, but he plays that horse trader role pretty good. And just to look at him, who would ever suspect that he's really who he is?"

Doc paused in his manipulations and picked up his glass of wine, which sat on a table by the bed. Nellie rolled over on her side, her blouse twisted and disheveled around her, and reached for her glass.

"We've been moving around so much lately, it's nice to just be able to lay around for a little while," Nellie said. She took a sip of her wine, then set it aside and lay back on the bed with her eyes closed. Doc studied the gentle rise and fall of her breasts as she breathed. He couldn't figure her out. He sensed that she might be available to him, but only if he turned just the right key to unlock her passions. He had felt a certain yearning in that single kiss he had stolen the night of the shoot-out, but since then she had refused all his advances with a combination of good humor and cynicism.

"I can almost feel your eyes on me," Nellie said softly, not opening her eyes to look at him.

"There's plenty to look at, and I like what I'm seeing," Doc told her.

"Where are you looking now?" she asked, as if they were playing some game.

"Guess."

Her hand stole up to her breast. As she touched it, her nipple pushed against the thin fabric of her clothing. She covered it with her fingers and Doc covered her hand with his.

"I feel so relaxed, Doc," she said. "I feel so good. Maybe it's the wine."

"And the massage," Doc suggested.

"That too. Your hands really know what they're doing."

"And they know what they like." When he reached for her other breast, and she did not resist, his fingers sought her nipple beneath the covering of her blouse and camisole. They found it eager to receive his caress.

"This is hardly a professional way for either of us to conduct ourselves," Nellie protested gently.

"Give yourself the day off from your duties," Doc said. "I did."

"But Frank might show up," she said.

"We're supposed to meet him for supper, but that's three hours from now." Doc's fingers were very slowly opening the buttons of her blouse, prolonging the pleasure of the act. Nellie reached up as if to stop him, but didn't. She watched as he folded the front panels of the blouse open, then sighed as his hands covered the soft mounds of flesh beneath the camisole.

"Doc, I just think that—"

He silenced her with a kiss. Her lips were as he remembered them, soft, communicating a subtle, sensuous message more eloquently than words possibly could. His lips roamed down across her neck and throat, seeking out the secret places that heightened her arousal. His hands fumbled with the camisole, frustrated by their seeming inability to either raise it up or pull it down.

"They know what they like, but they just can't figure how to get there, huh?" Nellie giggled.

"That damned thing is definitely in the way," Doc said.

Laughing lightly, Nellie sat up and slipped off her blouse, then pulled the camisole free from the waistband of her skirt and took it off over her head. Her breasts bobbed into view, their nipples rosy and enticing. "Satisfied?" she asked.

"You might as well keep going," Doc suggested.

"And what about you?" she asked.

The request needed no repeating. Doc rose at the side of the bed and undressed. He folded each garment neatly over the back of a nearby chair as he took it off. Nellie slipped out of her skirt, bloomers, and underwear, then lay back on the bed waiting for him to finish. She didn't seem the slightest bit embarrassed by her nudity, and in fact she had nothing at all to be ashamed of. Her body was even more splended than Doc had imagined it in his frequent daydreams about her recently. Her breasts mounded up with firm magnificence even as she lay on her back. Her waist was slender and girlish, and the wispy hint of hair between her legs was the same color and consistency as her blond tresses. Her legs were long and straight, as shapely and smooth as any Doc had seen.

In the brief moment that Doc stood gazing down at her, his cock began to thicken and rise. Nellie giggled at the immediacy of his reaction and reached out to stroke his organ admiringly. Her soft attentions made him shiver with pleasure.

"Well, are you going to stand there all day?" she asked.

"If you keep doing that, I might," he told her.

He stretched out beside her on the bed. Their bodies made warm contact from chest to thigh. As their lips joined, Doc's hands sampled the luxury of her flesh. His head dropped down to taste the tip of first one breast, then the other. Soft sounds of delight stirred from Nellie's throat, and she closed her eyes, savoring his attentions. One of her hands stayed busy between his legs, tracing the length of his cock with soft fingertips and gently caressing his testicles. Her touch was maddening and delightful.

"Your hands and lips know just exactly what I like," Nellie sighed. "I guess you get a lot of practice at this sort of thing."

"Not as much as I'd like to have," Doc told her. "I'm pretty selective about my women." He grazed his finger lightly down against her cunt, attempting to distract her, but she was not yet ready to simply relax and enjoy. She had something to say.

"I'm not just an easy conquest, Doc," she told him. "I haven't lived my whole life in a convent, but this sort of thing isn't common for me either."

"So you're selective too," Doc said. "That's good. That should make this all the more special for both of us."

"I want it to be special," she said softly.

She winced with pleasure as his finger probed gently into her, sampling the silky texture of her moist womanhood. She was beginning to settle in with the experience, putting doubts and uncertainties away and permitting herself to simply enjoy at last. Her fingers dabbed at the moisture that had appeared at the end of his cock, spreading it along the length of his shaft and lubricating her caresses. Doc could feel her heart pounding in her chest, matching the drumbeat of his own.

When he could stand it no longer, Doc spread her legs wide and positioned himself above her. As Nellie's hand went down to guide him toward her waiting quim, she looked him straight in the eye. Her smile was calm. He slid

her slowly, enjoying every delicious second as his flesh
ntered hers.

"Ummmmmm," Nellie sighed. "That's just right."

"I have to agree," Doc told her quietly. He pulled back
ome then moved forward again, heightening the sensations
or both of them.

"I've been wanting this as much as you," Nellie admitted
 him. "But I wanted it to be just right before it happened.
ot just some fumbling trailside tumble."

"It's just right now," Doc told her.

Though he was fully aroused by then, Doc felt no over-
owering sense of urgency about what he was doing. His
rokes were smooth and prolonged, probing each time to
e utmost depths within her before beginning the journey
ack out again. Nellie's passion was like a fire that grew
eadily and persistently until it blazed with unquenchable
tensity. In the end it was she, not he, who quickened the
ace to a frenzied urgency. Her sighs became chesty moans
 the first spasms of her orgasm gripped her.

Doc stayed with her during the entire thing, meeting the
ger demands of her pelvis with his steady thrusts, keeping
eir sweat-slickened bodies locked together as she bucked
d tossed wildly under him. When her ragged breathing
ally slowed and the violent arching of her body subsided,
 sucked in a great lungful of air, held it, and began to
me. The inside of her quim twitched and quivered as he
led her with his hot male juices.

"Oh, Doc! That was marvelous!" Nellie announced
eathlessly from beneath him. "If I had known it was going
 be that good, I'm not sure I could have waited this long."

"Maybe the wait is what made it so good," Doc sug-
sted. Nestled within her, his dick had softened only par-
lly. He moved his crotch tentatively, testing his organ's
llingness to stay erect. He felt it start to swell and fill her
ce more. Sometimes it happened that way when his need
s great enough and his partner was woman enough.

"Again?" Nellie asked in surprise.

"Can you think of a better way to spend the rest of those three hours we have to kill?" he asked.

Raider lay on his back, staring up at the starlit sky. Lucy was down at the creek washing up, but he didn't feel like moving a muscle yet. He felt too good to move. A couple of minutes later Lucy came back and knelt by his side. She cleaned his cock with a damp cloth. Despite the coolness of the water, his organ stiffened in her hand.

"Oh, no you don't, Buster," she said, seeming to address his manhood directly. "You're getting a rest, whether you want it or not." Raider grinned at her.

"We have to get dressed now," Lucy said. "Cousin Jesse's been gone for more than two hours already. He'll be back anytime."

"We could just tell him we got hot and decided to take our clothes off," Raider teased.

"Yeah, and the second he saw us both buck-assed naked like this," she said, "he'd realize just exactly how hot we got."

"All right, woman," Raider conceded. "Anything to keep you happy." He reached wearily for his clothes.

When they were both dressed, Lucy poured Raider a cup of coffee from the pot beside the campfire and he spiked it from a pint bottle of whiskey he had purchased. He offered her some, but she declined.

It was a quiet, comfortable time. The sex had been great and Lucy seemed to be suffering no upsetting aftereffects as she had the first time they'd made love. She sat on the ground beside him with her hand resting gently on his leg, gazing into the dying flames of the fire. Her calm smile showed how good she felt.

When he heard the sound of a horse's hooves approaching the camp, Raider drew his revolver from the holster that lay on the ground beside him, though he knew who it would probably be. A minute later Jesse James emerged from the darkness and stopped his horse near the spot where Raider and Lucy's mounts were tethered. Raider put his weapon away.

"Is there any word?" Lucy asked her cousin.

After tying his horse off to the tether rope, Jesse turned his dark, suspicious gaze on the two of them. Lucy had removed her hand from Raider's leg but still sat close to him.

"I sent the wire off to Dulcinda," Jesse said, "and I got an answer back about an hour later. Frank said they haven't had any more luck than we have. He says they're going to rest up there for one more day and then push on toward Wichita as planned."

"If that's the case," Raider said, "then I don't see why we shouldn't go on into Emporia and give ourselves a day off too. We'd still be able to get to Wichita about the time they do, and I don't see much reason why we should be out here sleeping on the ground when we could have beds in town. Besides, I'm tired of this chuck you've brought along. All this salt pork is giving me the cramps, and I'd love to belly up to a two-inch steak and a mess of fried potatoes."

"I wouldn't trust staying in Emporia for even one night," Jesse said. "I'm too well known in this part of the state."

"Well, goddamn, your brother stays in towns," Raider said.

"Sure, but he's not the one that gets his face plastered all over the reward posters every time a bank gets held up," Jesse said. "Hell, they even got a new drawing of me out now that's got a beard on it like the one I'm wearing."

"But it doesn't look much like you, Jesse," Lucy offered quietly. "Remember, we saw that one on a tree near Grimsley?"

"I still won't risk it," Jesse insisted. "We'll go right on camping out until we get to Wichita. I'll feel safer there 'cause it's a bigger town. Until then, we go on checking out the towns like we have been and then getting the hell out."

"I guess I missed the vote that made you ramrod of this outfit, James," Raider said. "But I think it's time for a recount."

In the manner of an experienced gunfighter, Jesse James had calmly been preparing himself for action. He had turned until he was standing nearly sideways to Raider, his feet braced several inches apart, his right hand hanging free near the hilt of his .45. Raider glanced down at his own pistol on the ground, trying to gauge time elements.

"I got six votes that say we do it my way, Pink," Jesse said coldly.

"Not again!" Lucy exclaimed in disgust. "This is the third time in four days that you two have bristled up at each other like a couple of starving yard dogs fighting over a biscuit."

"Stay out of this, Lucy," Jesse warned.

"I will not stay out of it," Lucy said, rising and placing her body between them. "I don't know what the two of you are trying to prove, but I'm getting tired of it. Have you forgotten why we're here and why you two joined forces in the first place? Was it just so you'd have a chance to pump some lead into one another over some silly little squabble?"

"I'll be damned if I'll start taking orders from a lousy goddamn Pinkerton," Jesse growled.

"Excuse me all to hell for wanting to spend one night on a real goddamn bed," Raider retorted.

"I got a pretty good idea what you've been spending some of your nighttime hours on already," Jesse said, "and I'm none too happy about that, either. Seems like the reasons just keep stacking up why I need to kill you, Pink."

"Just stop it, Jesse!" Lucy shouted. "And you too, Raider. We're here for a reason, and there's bound to be some way

hat the two of you can get along until we get this job
inished. Then if you want to show each other what big,
ad hombres you are, I swear I won't try to stop you." She
ooked at each of them in turn, then asked, "All right? All
ight, Raider?"

"I did give my word back there in the cave," he admitted.
And I guess I want to get my hands on those bank robbers
orse than I want a piece of his hide."

"Jesse?" Lucy asked. "All right?"

With a snort of disgust, Jesse turned and uncinched his
addle.

Raider reached for his coffee cup instead of his gun. He
ook a swig. The day was not too far off, he realized with
mixed sense of dread and anticipation, when things would
o beyond Lucy's ability to stop them.

CHAPTER ELEVEN

Nellie was sitting at a small writing table across the room when Doc awoke. She wore only one of his silk shirts, buttoned partially up the front, and had rolled the sleeves up loosely. She was hard at work with pen and paper, pausing occasionally to nibble the end of the pen before scribbling down another thought.

Doc glanced at the window and judged by the angle of the sunlight spilling into the room that it was about eight in the morning. After supper the previous evening, he and Nellie had returned here to his room for a repeated bout of lovemaking. Later he had slept deeply, with the young reporter snuggled contentedly in the crook of his arm. Even this morning he still felt sated and content.

He raised up onto his elbow and watched Nellie work for a while. Finally she seemed to feel his eyes on her and turned to give him a bright smile. "Good morning, Doc," she said cheerily.

"Good morning. What are you doing?"

"Just writing some things down."

"You haven't forgotten your promise not to file a story until we say it's okay, have you?" he asked.

"These are only notes," Nellie assured him. "When I do get a chance to submit my account of all this, I don't want to leave out a single detail. It will read like a dime novel, but every word of it will be absolutely true. I'm sure to get that reporter's job after this."

"But not until the proper time," Doc said.

"Don't worry, Doc. I'll keep my promise." Laying her pen down and turning toward him, she added brightly, "And besides, after yesterday, I'm not in such a great hurry to part company with you and head back. I can think of a few very entertaining reasons to stay with you to the very end." She wore his shirt open nearly to her waist, exposing a delightful expanse of smooth cleavage. Doc felt a familiar stirring down under the covers.

"Now that you've brought up the subject of our togetherness," he said, "come here and let's discuss it."

Nellie went over and sat down on the edge of the bed beside him, then kissed him lightly on the lips. Doc opened the remaining three buttons at the bottom of the shirt and reached up to fill his hand with one of her breasts. Her flesh was cool, but warmed with his touch.

"I've never been on such a sexual binge in my life," she said. "I think I've lost count of how many times we've done it in the past eighteeen hours."

"After a famine or two," Doc reflected, "you learn to feast when there's plenty. Come here, woman."

Nellie melted willingly into his arms, but before she could shift around and slide under the cover with him, a knocked sounded on the door.

"Doc, it's me," Frank James said from outside.

Nellie looked at Doc in alarm, then glanced across the room to a connecting door that led to her room. "I'll make him wait if you want to gather your things and go in there," Doc told her quietly.

"I've got news," Frank said. "I think you'll want to hear this."

Nellie's curiosity overcame her modesty. "I'll stay," she decided, shifting around on the bed and pulling the covers up around her like a robe. Doc got up and pulled his trousers on, then went over to let his visitor in.

When Frank James entered the hotel room he glanced at the two of them with an amused look on his face, but he made no comment. Nellie blushed and pulled the blanket a little more tightly around her.

"So what's the news?" Doc asked. He fished an Old Virginia cheroot from the pocket of his jacket and lit it with a lucifer.

"I was out early for breakfast this morning," Frank announced, "and on the way back to the hotel, I spotted a man that I'm pretty sure I recognized."

"Is that significant?" Doc asked, not yet understanding the other man's enthusiasm.

"If he's the man I think he is, his name is Dudley Gleason. He was a small-time horse thief and highwayman before the war. I first met him when I joined up with Quantrill. Near the end of the war, when the raiders began to split up, he headed south with a few others who decided they'd rather go down and be bandits along the Mexican border than stick around these parts and fight to the end."

"And you figure he might still be in the same line of work?" Doc suggested.

"Knowing Gleason, it seems likely," Frank said. "If it was him. I followed him down the street a ways, but when he went in a saloon I decided not to follow him in and risk being recognized. Instead I came back here to get you to help me."

"Give me a minute to get dressed," Doc said, opening his bag for a fresh shirt.

Frank James was waiting across the street when Doc emerged from the saloon nearly an hour later. Doc joined him, and the two of them walked back to the hotel.

"He's using the name Sam Dudley now," Doc announced, "but I'd bet anything he's the same man. After I got him primed with about half a bottle of rye, he got to talking about all the rough times he'd seen during the war. He never did mention Quantrill, but it was easy to tell his sympathies had been with the South."

"It's got to be Gleason, but what's he doing here? Did you find out?"

"Well, he told me he worked for a rancher hereabouts," Doc said. "Somebody named Harry Smolett."

"Smolett!" Frank James said. He spoke the name as if it left a bad taste in his mouth. "I'll be damned."

"Then you know this Harry Smolett?" Doc asked.

"I know Hank Smolett," the outlaw explained bitterly. "If he hadn't left for Texas when he did back in '64, either he or I would be planted in a pine box today."

"It sounds like we might really have something here," Doc said with rising enthusiasm. "The thing to do now, it seems, is to check out this Smolett. But if he's got a ranch in this area and is living a respectable sort of life now, it'll be difficult to pin a bank robbery on him."

"It's the respectable ones you've got to watch out for sometimes," Frank James quipped. "A neat suit and a little superficial gentility can cover up quite a bit."

"I see what you mean," Doc said. That philosophy had certainly served the James brothers well. "I guess we'd better take a close look at this Smolett fellow."

Doc let Judith set her own plodding pace across the dry Kansas prairie. Small farmsteads surrounded by fields of knee-high wheat and corn were scattered randomly along both sides of the road, but much of the country remained open range. Gusts of hot wind assaulted him occasionally, and tumbleweeds rushed busily across his path on their way to nowhere. Cattle grazed in clots on the sparse grasses.

A shopkeeper in Dulcinda had told him that Smolett's ranch, the Falling S, was about five miles out of town, but Doc felt as if he had driven the wagon twice that distance before he finally reached the turnoff. When he came to it at last, Doc stopped in the middle of the main road and had a look.

A weathered sign was suspended across the rutted side road with the aid of two tall poles. Peeling twelve-inch letters emblazoned across the sign announced that this was indeed the Falling S, and below, in smaller letters, was the warning "TRESPASSERS WILL BE SHOT."

"Do you think they mean us, Judith?" Doc said, addressing the mule. "Surely not." He gave her reins a tug, turning her left down the side road. In the distance, a cluster of matchbox buildings shimmered and danced on heat waves, growing larger only in imperceptible degrees.

After a few minutes, Doc watched as a couple of dark dots separated themselves from the ranch buildings and started in his direction. Gradually they transformed themselves into two mounted men. Doc continued his progress until the men got close enough to block the way with their horses.

"You break your glasses, mister?" one of the men asked gruffly. He was a huge, brutish fellow with a wiry black beard and dark, threatening eyes.

"If you're referring to that sign back by the road," Doc told him calmly, "I didn't consider myself a trespasser. Not precisely."

"Well pree-cisely," the second man said, mimicking Doc's manner of speech, "what the shit do you consider yourself?" By the crooked, mocking grin on his face, Doc judged him to be the wiseass of the Falling S crew.

"I am Dr. Weatherbee," Doc announced, "purveyor of homeopathic medicines and nostrums for all manner of ailments which commonly afflict man or beast alike."

"A tonic doctor, huh?" the second man said. "Wal, you risked a bullet fer nothin' here, mister. Everybody on this spread is too ornery to get sick." He chuckled at his own witticism, but his companion did not join him in the laughter. A sense of humor did not seem to be a part of the larger man's makeup.

"And I take it that your employer owns no cattle," Doc said.

"Huh?" the second man asked. "O' course we got cattle. How can you have a damn ranch without cows?"

"Well, sir, if this is a ranch with cattle, then I suggest that you let your employer decide whether or not my presence is welcome here, rather than taking the responsibility upon yourselves. Now, with the epidemic spread as far east as Páwnee County, it would seem imperative that—"

"Epidemic?" the man asked. "What epidemic?"

"Why, the slavering doldrums," Doc exclaimed in surprise. "I thought that surely even the ranchers in this area had been warned of it by now."

"Listen, Doctor," the man responded with alarm. "We haven't heard a peep about this slobbering whatever-you-said. What's it all about?"

"As near as we know, the first herds heading up out of Texas this spring must have brought it with them. In its early stages in cattle it is characterized by myopia and excessive salivary activity, and if left untreated usually results in olfactory paralysis and death."

"Death, huh?" the man said, clinging to the one word he understood.

"Unlike the hardier Texas breeds, the great majority of Kansas cattle seem to have no immunity to the disease," Doc explained.

"Goddamn Texans," the burly cowboy growled. "First they bring us the anthrax, and now this."

"Fortunately, there is a simple cure for the slavering doldrums," Doc told them on a brighter note. "That's why I'm here now. To take your employer's order for the necessary amounts of vaccine."

The two men looked at one another, no doubt wondering whether they should still evict Doc from the ranch. "Smolett said run him off," the larger man reminded his companion.

"But shit!" the other man said. "He hadn't heard nothin' about this epidemic either. The boss owns nearly three hundred head of cattle, an' he's gonna need some of that vaccine."

"A'right, Smiley," the big man said. "But if he blows his boiler, it's on your head."

"Right, Bruno."

Smiley and Bruno, Doc thought. The names fit.

In a moment Bruno turned back to Doc and asked, "You totin' iron, mister?"

Doc rolled his eyes at the cornball turn of phrase. "I've got a little revolver in back for snakes and varmints," he said.

"Wal, you just make sure it stays back there," Bruno warned. "Any critters get in your way while you're on Falling S land, we'll take care of 'em for you."

During the ten-minute ride to the ranch house, Doc went over in his mind the details of the ridiculous yarn he had made up for the benefit of the two cowboys, knowing he must tell it exactly the same way a second time to Smolett. For a moment he also considered hauling out his Primo Sr. camera once he arrived and offering to take a group shot of the rancher and his crew. Any photograph he could take would be invaluable in making positive identification of the bank robbers. But finally he discarded the idea as too risky. During this trip he didn't want to do or say anything that might arouse the suspicions of Smolett and his men.

There was nothing unusual about the layout of the headquarters area of the ranch. The main house was a substantial-looking white frame structure with a wide porch running the full width of its front. To the rear was a long bunkhouse and a cook shack. A large barn, complete with corrals and assorted outbuildings, stood farther away behind.

What immediately struck Doc as odd, however, was that nobody around the place seemed to be working. A couple of men were perched on the top rail of one of the corrals near the barn, seeming to discuss the animals before them, and four more were reclining under a shade tree near the bunkhouse, smoking and passing a bottle around. They all began to gather near the front of the main house as Doc and his escort neared, and in a minute a man came out of the front door of the house and stopped on the edge of the porch.

"Damn you, Smiley Barnett!" the man on the porch stormed. "Didn't I tell you to turn that wagon around and head it back the way it came?"

Doc had to force himself not to gawk in open amazement at the man he presumed to be Harry Smolett. With a heavy beard covering the lower portion of his face and a certain distinctive look of malice in his eye, he looked enough like Jesse James to be his brother. The height and weight were both about right too, and Smolett wore his revolver slung low on his right hip in the manner of a seasoned gunslinger, just like Jesse.

"That's what you said, boss," Smiley said, "but this feller here, he says—"

"I don't want to hear no goddamn spiel from no goddamn peddler," Smolett erupted. "Listen, dude," he added, addressing Doc. "Whatever you got to sell, we don't need any, an' if you figure your hide's worth something more than half an ounce of hot lead, you'll turn that wagon around and haul it off my land like the devil was after you."

"It's about the cattle," Smiley explained hastily, "an' the slobber epidemic."

"What?" Smolett asked, turning to his man with a look of incredulity on his face. "The *what* epidemic?"

"More precisely put, sir," Doc said. "My visit here concerns the epidemic of slavering doldrums which the Texas trail herds brought north with them this spring." Quickly he repeated the preposterous tale he had told the two hands earlier, though he could tell that it failed to stir the same alarm in the ranch owner.

"I never heard such a crock of shit in all my born days!" Smolett proclaimed when Doc was finished. "I think this is just some stupid line you're handing me to sell me some kind of bullshit tonic and cure-alls."

"Believe what you want, Mr. Smolett," Doc replied disdainfully. "But I have nothing with me to sell and I'm not asking for a cent of your money today. I'm simply taking orders for the vaccine. More than anything else, I consider my work a public service for those who wish to take advantage of it."

He could tell Smolett wasn't buying any of it. A look of cold amusement crept into the rancher's eye as he drew his revolver. "Tell me something, root peddler," Smolett said, pointing the gun at Doc. "Have you got yourself any vaccine for the sickness that one of these serves up?"

"I assure you there is no call for violence," Doc told him, affecting the nervousness of a very frightened man. Under the circumstances, it was not a difficult role to play. "I am quite willing to leave immediately."

"That's just barely soon enough," Smolett sneered.

Doc turned the wagon and drove away. He heard the rancher cursing and reviling the two men who had let him in. Doc chuckled to himself as he clicked Judith into a faster gait. Stupidity such as theirs was often its own punishment.

CHAPTER TWELVE

"Time I was six, Mama and I were pretty much on our own," Lucy was saying. "Papa lit out for Mexico in '63 when he heard they were coming around to take him away in the army. Years later we heard he'd got his throat slit by a whore in Monterrey, but by then it didn't matter much to either of us. I don't hardly remember him now, except as that scary man I had to hide from once or twice a month when he got liquored up. Once, I remember, he beat Mama up, and after he passed out, she took a claw hammer and broke his right hand. He behaved himself after that until he went away."

Lucy rode a horse as well as most men Raider knew. She had the easy grace of a woman who had lived as much of her life in a saddle as she had with her feet on the ground.

"We had this little place outside Austin," she said. "Just a few head of horses and never any more than two dozen cows. It was enough for us to live on, but just barely enough. Two days a week, Mama would go into town and clean house for a banker named Jessup. That's how she kept the mortgage paid. After I got older she started sleeping over there sometimes, and then I realized what was going on. They didn't ever fall in love with each other, but I guess it was convenient. They both got something they needed, and I couldn't see much blame in it."

The road west into Broadway was lined with neat little farms, each with its two-or three-room white frame house, garden plot, milk cow, chickens, and children. Something about the orderliness of the area appealed to Raider. People here were doing what they were supposed to be doing, tending to their own lives and making a decent job of it.

"Frank and Jesse were more like uncles to me than cousins when I was little," Lucy explained. "In the early days after the war, they'd show up once or twice a year down where we lived. They'd spend a couple of weeks mending fences and patching holes in the roof. Things like that. Then when they left, it seemed like for a while there was money for a few extras that we couldn't afford the rest of the year."

"It would be hard to think bad about kinfolks like that," Raider admitted.

"Oh, I knew they were famous outlaws even back then," she said. "I understood real young that I couldn't ever tell anybody who they were or they'd get in a lot of trouble. But the idea I always had in my head was that they stole money from bad men, and that anybody they killed must be a damn Yankee and needed killing. Even when I got older and really knew better, that impression of them stuck in my head. I still can't look at them and think of them as bad men. I just can't do it."

They were approaching a stand of trees several acres in

size, a rarity in these parts. If there was water there, Raider thought, it might be a good place to stop and let the horses drink. Suddenly the sense of urgency that he had been feeling over the past few days was gone. It was a beautiful afternoon, the kind of day when a man should take his time about things, and now that they were away from Jesse and out on their own for a few hours, he was in no hurry to return to camp.

"Mama's getting old, so about six months ago we sold the place and got her a little house in town. Then this last time when Frank and Jesse came to see us, they offered to take me along with them when they came back this way. I got this crazy notion in my head that I could join their gang and become a famous woman outlaw, you know, like Belle Starr or somebody."

"I got a look at Belle Starr one time," Raider said. "She had a face that would curdle milk, and she smelled so bad a man couldn't hardly stand to be in the same room with her. But maybe it was one of her off times. I don't know."

"Well, it's the idea of somebody like that, and not who they really are," Lucy tried to explain. "It's the notion that you grow up with about high times and adventure and plenty of money after a big stickup."

"Sometimes it's a long ways from being the truth," Raider noted.

"Frank's been trying to tell me about that," she said. "Jesse loves it, plain out. It's like he was made to live the exact life he's living now. But sometimes when Frank talks about how it is to shoot a man or to get shot, and when he tells about being on the run and not knowing whether he'll ever see his family again, I know it's different with him."

"But he's stuck with it now," Raider said, "until the day finally comes when—"

"When somebody like you ends it for him."

"Probably."

"Could you shoot him, Raider?" Lucy asked. "After all

this, could you really just take out your gun and kill either one of them?"

"I wouldn't rule out the possibility," Raider told her quietly.

They entered the trees in silence. A few dozen yards away a creek snaked its way through the underbrush. Raider dropped the reins of his horse, letting the animal make its own way to the water. Lucy led hers over to the creek before turning it loose.

Out of habit, Raider took a moment to look both ways down the road, searching for he didn't know what. Then he joined Lucy at the edge of the creek, slipping his arm casually around her waist.

"I guess, in spite of everything," she said, "you and I are still supposed to be enemies." She leaned her head against Raider's shoulder more gently than any enemy should.

"Only if you think it's necessary to take sides in this thing," he told her. "You've never broken the law, have you, Lucy? Have you ever robbed a bank or put a bullet in the belly of a train conductor?"

"I guess I haven't," she admitted.

"Then we don't have to be enemies unless you decide to be," he said.

They stood there for a while, listening to the ripple of the water over the rocks, enjoying the chirps of a few birds who had paused nearby to investigate the intruders in their sanctuary.

"Them horses look fagged." Raider said at last.

"How could they be?" Lucy asked. "We haven't been riding a full hour, and we've walked them all the way."

"They look plumb wore out to me," Raider insisted. "Damned if it wouldn't be downright inhuman to push them any farther before they've had a rest." When Lucy looked up at him, the twinkle in his eye explained everything.

"Horny bastard!" She laughed.

Raider loosened the blanket on the back of his saddle

and spread it on a level spot of ground beneath the trees. When the horses had finished drinking, they found a patch of grass beside the creek and began to graze contentedly.

He removed his gunbelt and laid it carefully on the edge of the blanket, then began unbuttoning his shirt. But he stopped when Lucy sat down in the middle of the blanket, making no move to take her own clothes off.

"What's the matter?" Raider asked. "Don't you feel like it?"

"I just want to watch," she said, smiling up at him.

"Watch what?"

"I want to watch you take your clothes off, Raider."

"What in the hell for?" he asked. "You've seen me naked before. A couple of times. Nothing's changed since last time."

"Haven't you ever enjoyed watching a woman undress? Well, it's the same thing here, but just turned around on you. I'll enjoy it."

Raider felt a sudden, ridiculous wave of embarrassment. His fingers hesitated over a button midway down his shirt.

"Come on, big boy," Lucy teased. "Let's see your stuff."

"Christ A'mighty!" Raider exclaimed, nearly ripping his shirt from his body. "You want me to spin around like a high stepper too?" he growled. "Or will the up-front view be good enough for you?"

"Maybe you can turn around a couple of times for me later," she said, smiling wickedly. Her eyes caressed every portion of his body as it came into view—his husky shoulders, his broad chest, and his lean belly layered with muscle. Raider felt like some sort of sideshow freak on display behind a glass wall, but soon he started to realize that the situation was oddly stimulating, too. Hobbling around on one foot after the other, he tugged off his boots, then managed to shed his jeans with a little more grace. When he finished, he remained standing in front of her for a reaction.

Lucy moved toward him and raised up onto her knees,

caressing the side of one of his legs gently with her fingertips. "So many scars. My God," she murmured in awe. "It was always dark before. I've never noticed them so clearly."

"Sometimes it gets rough on a man in my line of work," Raider said.

"Just like with Frank and Jesse."

"Well, men in their line of work gave me most of these. In that way, I guess you could say it's the same. But it's not the same either."

She ran her hands down his shanks like a horse trader inspecting a potential purchase, then trailed her fingertips back up the insides of his legs. "Nice," she told him, admiring the shape and texture of his body. Then, as her hand settled over his rising organ, she said, "Very nice."

She kissed the end of his cock, then slowly settled her lips over its swollen head. Raider felt an immediate surge of pleasure race out from his groin to all parts of his body. She drew him into her mouth slowly, keeping her tongue active along the length of the delicate underflesh of his member. His knees felt weak, and he locked them to keep from staggering. She accepted him into her mouth until she reached the point of gagging, then pursed her lips and slowly withdrew. Raider shuddered. He twined his fingers loosely in her hair for balance, closed his eyes, and drifted with the feelings she was arousing.

Lucy was patient and gentle, taking full control, leading him slowly down the path toward fulfillment. When she sensed that he was about to come at last, she drew her mouth away and smiled up at him.

"Wow!" Raider told her dizzily. He fought for control, knowing what she wanted.

"Let's finish up the other way," she coaxed. Only when she spoke did Raider realize how breathlessly excited she had become. She was out of her clothes in an instant, lying back on the blanket with her legs spread, eager to receive him.

Almost as soon as he slid into her, Raider felt the urge to climax surging once more. He held it as long as he was able, which wasn't very long. But as soon as he began to gasp and thrust uncontrollably, he could feel Lucy shuddering into her own finish beneath him. She locked her legs around him and wouldn't let him stop even when his body began to feel as drained and lifeless as one of the mossy logs around them. Repeated spasms of delight racked her body, and she filled the woods with her prolonged moans. Raider felt a definite sense of relief when she had finally taken all she could stand.

Lucy's legs fell away to the sides and her eyes sagged shut. Perspiration beaded her upper lip and forehead, and the breath raced in and out of her mouth raggedly. When Raider moved to withdraw from her, he could feel the muscles inside her convulse in a series of aftershocks.

"That's some good fucking, Mr. Pinkerton Man," she panted.

"We're some enemies, aren't we?" he responded.

Raider held a yellow telegraph slip in his hand when he came out of the Broadway Western Union office. As he stepped into the street, he waved it so Lucy could see it from where she waited in front of a dry goods store.

"This is it!" he told her enthusiastically. "They've spotted some suspects in Dulcinda and they want us to join them there."

"Let me see," Lucy said excitedly. Raider handed her the telegram and she read it quickly, then looked up at Raider with an unexpectedly serious look on her face.

"What's the matter?" Raider asked her. "This is the break we've been waiting for. We're on our way."

"We're on our way," she agreed. " But what happens when we get there?"

"We nail these shitheads to the smokehouse door, that's what."

"And then?"

Raider knew that the young woman's thoughts were still on the possible confrontation between the two Pinkertons and her outlaw relatives after the bank robbers had been dealt with, but he had no reassurance to give her. He honestly didn't know what would happen when that moment arrived.

"We'll deal with that when the time comes," he told her. "But first things first. Right now we've got to carry this news to your cousin Jesse and point ourselves toward Dulcinda. If we ride hard all night, we can be there by noon tomorrow."

The small hotel room was crowded and hot, and the smoke from Doc's cigar didn't improve the quality of the air any. Finally, to Raider's great relief, Nellie Rosemond took the cheroot from Doc's mouth and stubbed it out in an ashtray. The possessiveness of her gesture didn't escape Raider's notice, nor did Doc's acceptance of what she did.

"Here's what we've got so far," Doc was explaining to the new arrivals. "We've got a former Confederate renegade and border bandit suddenly turned respectable rancher in a small town in Kansas. He looks enough like Jesse James to pass for him with a mask over his face, and he's got at least enough men working for him to have pulled the Fidelity National robbery.

"The distances are no problem. On good mounts, they could reach Kansas City from here in two days, and they probably know the country in between pretty well. Since the search for the robbers was concentrated north of the city instead of south, it's not unreasonable to believe that they could have made it back this far without being spotted.

"As far as descriptions go," Doc continued "it's hard to nail anything down concretely. People tend to get details all mixed up in their minds in crisis situations like a robbery, but at least a couple seem to fit pretty closely. There's a description of an unusually large man with a black beard nd a killer look in his eyes, and another of a man with ong blond hair and a slanting scar across his forehead. I aw two men with those characteristics at Smolett's ranch."

"Whitey Tunes?" Frank James wondered, glancing over t his brother. "He didn't wear his hair long during the war, ut he did have a scar like that from a Yankee saber slash."

"Sure, I remember Whitey had a scar on his forehead," esse recollected. "And what was the name of that big ugly astard that only rode with us a couple of months back in 63 or '64? Remember, Bill Anderson run him off after he aped those two farm girls and then . . ." He hesitated, glanc-ng at the two women, and did not finish the statement. The one Bill kicked out."

"Could it possibly be Bruno something?" Doc asked.

"Bruno?" Jesse reflected.

"Yeah, that's it," Frank exclaimed. "Remember, Jesse? t was Bruno Jakes. Boy, old Hank Smolett's sure put him-elf together one hell of a crew out there. Dudley Gleason, Bruno Jakes, Whitey Tunes . . ."

"Every one of 'em so low they'd have to reach up to kill snake," Jesse said. "And I bet we'd know half the rest of hem if we got a look at them, too."

"But just 'cause they're skunks doesn't mean they're the kunks we're after," Raider reminded the brothers. "What lse have you got, Doc?"

"Nothing strong enough to take to a jury, I'm afraid," Doc said. "I talked to the banker here in Dulcinda, and he aid Smolett paid off the rest of the mortgage on his place arly this week. And a couple of bartenders in town indi-ated that Smolett's men always seemed to have plenty of oins jingling in their pockets."

"They're the ones," Jesse said firmly. "By God, I know t!"

"I'm as certain as you are," Frank agreed with conviction. They're the ones."

"Just 'cause you want them to be the ones so bad?" Raider

asked. "A judge won't likely hang none of them on the strength of your hunches."

"You don't know the whole story," Frank explained patiently. "There's more than guesswork going on here." He looked at his brother questioningly. Jesse nodded.

"It was in '64, right after we massacred Johnson and a hundred or so Yankee soldiers down at Centralia," Frank explained further. "By then the bluebellies were pushing us hard everywhere we went, and the guerrillas were split up most of the time, spending more time running and hiding then doing any real fighting. Jesse and I were riding with a group under Bloody Bill Anderson, heading northwest toward Independence. We figured to rest up awhile, then head south and join up with General Shelby's regulars. We were all jittery as rattlers, not sure who we could trust or what direction we could go to keep our tails out of a sling. Most of us were just about used up by then, and we could smell the end coming."

"But Smolett, that piece of barnyard slime," Jesse added, "knew where he was headed. He had his sights set on Texas, but he wanted some folding money in his pockets to carry along. So he sold us out. He set up Frank and me and two others."

"Hank Smolett came to us one night," Frank continued, "and he told us the Yankees had Anderson and a couple of others trapped in a little farmhouse a couple of miles away. But he said there were only a half dozen Yankees there and we could handle them easy if we came up through the trees behind them. Well, we fell for it. We came to find out that Bill wasn't there, but the Yankees sure were. Thirty of them."

"One of them got jittery and sprung the trap a minute too soon," Jesse said. "Their plan was to catch us in a crossfire, but one of their green troopers started shooting too soon, and we were able to turn around and get out in time."

"I put a bullet in Smolett that night," Frank said. "I thought for sure I'd killed him, but about five years later I came across him down in Texas. I went after him, but he put the Texas Rangers on me that time before I could catch up to him. I just barely got out of the state in one piece."

"Sounds like a fine friend to have," Raider drawled. "In Quantrill's outfit, I bet you couldn't throw a stick ten feet without hitting a feller like that."

"Look, you!" Jesse James said, bristling at the remark and half rising from his seat. Frank halted him with a hand on his arm.

"Just like any other organization, we had our heroes and our scoundrels," Frank said coldly. "And we had our share of jackassed loudmouths, too."

Doc sniggered, and Raider wasn't sure what direction to aim his scowl in, so he just scanned the room with it.

"None of this is putting us any closer to a plan of action," Doc reminded the others.

"Well, I just wanted the two of you to know how it was between us and Smolett," Frank explained. "It fits right in that he might decide to take up bank robbery posing as the James Gang."

"I think it's time to send for the backup, Doc," Raider announced with conviction. "The old man can be here with an army in less than a day, and then we'll go out there and turn Smolett's place upside down. Even if we don't find the money or evidence that they took the bank, I'll bet there's still fugitive warrants out on him and two-thirds of his crew."

"Now wait just a goddamn minute here!" Jesse James exclaimed. "What's this talk about you calling in your people?"

"How else will we take Smolett and his crew?" Raider asked. "Do you think Doc and I should ride out by ourselves and arrest the lot of them? Or maybe you and Frank would like to be in on the arrest."

"I had some quicker justice in mind," Jesse said.

"We agreed that you wouldn't contact your people until everybody consented," Frank reminded Raider and Doc.

"But don't you think we have to adapt to the situation as it is?" Doc reasoned. "I know that you two came here bent on revenge, but consider the numbers. And consider the fact that if we go out there undermanned and make a mess of things, Smolett and his crew are likely to scatter to the four winds before anybody else can get after them."

"Hanging would make them just as dead as a slug from your forty-five, James," Raider told Jesse.

Jesse started to protest again, but his brother interrupted him. "Maybe they're right, Jesse," he said.

"If they were, it'd be the first time," Jesse grumbled. "You know how we planned it, Frank. What are we supposed to do now? Just wait at the station and say howdy when Allan Pinkerton, his goddamn self, comes rolling in with three dozen special deputies along? I'd sooner kiss Abe Lincoln's ass."

"We'll have to disappear before they get here, of course," Frank said calmly. Neither Doc nor Raider quite understood the meaning of the looks that passed back and forth between the outlaw brothers, but suddenly Jesse stopped arguing. He slumped down in his chair to brood and grumble beneath his breath.

"I suppose it's up to you two to do what you think you must now," Frank told the Pinkertons. "But you know that as soon as you send out that telegram, you can't count on us for support any longer."

"So be it, then," Doc agreed. Frank and Doc seemed on the verge of shaking hands with one another, but the gesture somehow didn't seem appropriate. Frank turned to the door and Jesse rose to join him. Somewhat more reluctantly, Lucy got up. Her eyes were filled with questions and yearnings as they fell on Raider for an instant.

"Even if I send the telegram out right away, you'll still

be safe in town for several more hours," Doc said as the three were preparing to leave.

Raider met Lucy's gaze. "We'll probably have supper at the Prairie View about the same time," he said.

But it was Frank James who responded. "The Prairie View," he said as they left the hotel room. "All right."

CHAPTER THIRTEEN

The supper table resembled some sort of gastronomic battleground, especially in the vicinity of where Raider was sitting. The two-pound steak he had ordered was now reduced to a T-shaped bone and a few slivers of fat. Likewise, the platter that had contained his double order of fried potatoes and hot rolls was now vacant, and less than an inch of beer remained in the pitcher near his place. The buttons on the lower portion of Raider's plaid shirt were bearing nearly all the strain they could tolerate.

"I wouldn't have believed it if I hadn't seen it," Nellie commented, glancing at the carnage in front of Raider.

"He just makes a pig of himself like that for my benefit," Doc grumbled. "He knows how it irritates me to have people all over a respectable eating establishment turning in their chairs to watch him gorge himself like a starving orphan."

Raider restrained the urge to belch out of deference to Nellie.

"It's no wonder you have so much stomach trouble," Doc carped. "No man's insides are designed to hold that much bulk at one time." Then turning back to Nellie, he added, "But I have my brief moments of revenge." He took a cheroot from the breast pocket of his gray suit jacket and inspected it with pleasure before putting it in his mouth.

"Doc, you're not going to light one of those stinking things now, are you?" Raider scowled. "One whiff will spoil the best meal I've squared off to in a month."

"You could always go outside while I smoke," Doc suggested.

"I think I'll need a couple of minutes before I can get up from the table," Raider said, patting his stomach.

Nellie sat back, listening to their banter, realizing how harmless it was. In idle moments, their constant bickering and insults seemed to be their way of expressing their friendship for one another.

Doc's first puff of smoke drifted across the table, assaulting Raider's nostrils and prompting him to growl, "If there wasn't a lady here with us, I'd give you my idea of where I'd love to stuff that stinking roll of goat droppings."

"You're welcome to try it," Doc commented casually. "As soon as you're able to stand."

"I wonder why the others didn't show up," Nellie said, interrupting their exchanges at last. "It would have been nice to spend a hour or so with them before we all went our separate ways."

"I can think of a lot of folks in this world I'd rather chow down with than Jesse James," Raider said. "That brother of his didn't seem to be such a bad sort, though, for an owlhoot." Then he added, somewhat self-consciously, "And I guess I wouldn't have minded saying bye to their cousin."

"They must have decided to put some miles behind them efore the old man got here," Doc suggested. "And that light not be such a bad idea, when you think about it. If llan Pinkerton got here and learned that the James brothers vere close by, it might be a toss-up who he'd go after, them r the bank robbers."

"There'll be another time," Raider said. "All the way ver here, every time I looked at that Jesse James, I kept etting this feeling that someday, someplace . . ."

"You two didn't get on so well, did you?" Doc said.

"Like vinegar and baking soda."

"But things went a little smoother with Lucy, huh?" ellie teased. Raider held his tongue.

After their meal, Doc decided to walk down and check 1 Judith, and for want of something better to do, Raider ent with him. Nellie returned to the hotel.

As Doc was getting a measure of oats for his mule, Raider anced around the dim interior of the livery barn and was ildly surprised to see that the outlaws had left behind the /o horses they had acquired near Caseyville for him and ellie to ride.

"Probably stolen anyway," Raider mumbled to himself.

But then he was even more surprised to look over and e that Lucy's horse was there too, still in the stall next his where he had put it when he brought the horses to e stable hours earlier. Frank and Jesse's horses were both ne.

"Doc, come over here," Raider called out. "See what u make of this."

As soon as Doc saw the horse, he said, "I don't like it, de."

"What do you think it means? You figure they lied to ?"

"Well, if they were honest men, they wouldn't be in the e of work they've chosen," Doc said. "I think the pos-ilities are good that they pulled one over on us."

While they were still discussing the situation, they heard the back door of the livery barn scrape open. The door was just out of their line of sight, and something made Doc and Raider step back into the shadows of the stall until they could see who had come in. Raider drew his revolver a cautious footsteps came their way.

Lucy Samuels was just as startled as the two Pinkerton when she reached the stall and saw them. "Raider! Doc! was just . . . I mean . . ." she stammered. She held a full pack in her hand, but set it on the floor as Raider came over to her. She was obviously agitated.

"What in the hell's going on here?" Raider demanded "What's in the pack?"

"Just food and supplies for the trail," she told him. He inspected the pack briefly and saw that it contained what she claimed.

"So what's going on, Lucy?" Raider repeated.

"Frank and Jesse rode on ahead," Lucy explained nervously, "and I stayed behind to buy some supplies. I'm going to catch up with them on the trail."

"That doesn't make much sense," Doc said, advancing to stand by his partner. "Why would they leave you behind to buy supplies when they could just as easily do it themselves before they left?"

"It's a pretty lame story, Lucy," Raider said.

"Jesse got nervous. He started worrying that he might be recognized, so he and Frank went on ahead."

"And left you behind to face whatever danger might arise by yourself," Doc suggested.

"You're going to have to do better than that, girl," Raider said. "They went out to Smolett's, didn't they?"

She could see that it wasn't any use lying anymore. He story was a ridiculous one, and the two detectives had guessed the truth easily.

"I'm supposed to meet them outside town after they go through at the ranch," Lucy admitted at last. "They said would probably be midnight or later."

"Do they honestly expect to take on Smolett's whole crew by themselves?" Raider asked in amazement. "They're good, but no two men are that good. And the ones they're going up against aren't exactly amateurs themselves."

"They're not going to try to kill everybody," she explained. "They decided they would just try to get their hands on Smolett and make him tell them where the money was. Then they were going to kill him and go. He's the leader, and he's the one they wanted to get their revenge on. They said they'd leave the cleanup for you two."

"Damn their lying hides anyway!" Raider exclaimed, turning away from Lucy toward Doc. "I guess we haven't got much choice in the matter, do we, partner?"

"It looks like we have to go on out there, whether we want to or not," Doc agreed.

"I'll saddle the horses while you head back to the hotel and gather up whatever you think we'll need," Raider said. "Don't forget to bring my carbine with you, and all the extra cartridges you can find in my saddlebags. Damn it all anyway!"

"While I'm there I'll tell Nellie to alert the sheriff to what's going on. Maybe he can round up some sort of posse and come along behind us."

After Doc was gone, Raider located their saddles and gear and began preparing two of the horses for riding. In the stall where her horse was, Lucy was doing the same thing.

"You're not coming with us," Raider said when he realized what she was up to.

"The hell I'm not!" Lucy said defiantly.

"We're going to have enough problems out there without having some skirt to watch out over," Raider told her. "You can either stay here or head out to where you were supposed to meet them. Take your pick."

"I've already taken my pick, Raider. If Cousin Frank and

Cousin Jesse are in trouble, I'll be useful out there. I've been hunting with a rifle since I was eight years old, and I hit what I aim at. With you or by myself, I'm going."

Raider could see that there was no way he could stop her short of having her locked up in the town jail, which he didn't want to take the time to do.

"All right, dang it!" he growled at last. "You can ride out with us. But if we run head-on into trouble out there, you damned well better do what you're told."

"If there is trouble," Lucy assured him, "you won't regret having me along."

"Lucy, you bull-headed little hussy," Raider snapped at her. "I regret it already!"

CHAPTER FOURTEEN

They began to hear the shooting while they were still more than a mile from the Falling S headquarters. The gunfire was sporadic, but there was enough of it to show that things hadn't gone smoothly for the James brothers. Doc, Raider, and Lucy stopped their horses far down the access road to discuss what they should do now.

"We can't just go charging straight in," Doc said. "We won't know where Frank and Jesse are, and they probably wouldn't realize who we were either. I think we should circle around to the far side and try to slip up behind the barn. Smolett's men won't expect anybody to be coming in from that direction."

"And then what?" Raider asked.

"Maybe from the barn we'll be able to figure out where everybody is. We can decide from there."

"Well, I can't think of anything better," Raider said. "Let's do it your way."

They rode in a wide circle so they wouldn't be seen, keeping themselves oriented by the occasional shots fired in the distant cluster of buildings. The moon played games behind the clouds that dappled the sky, throwing the three riders alternately into revealing brightness and utter darkness. Eventually a moment of moonlight disclosed the nearness of the large barn a few hundred yards to their left.

"We'd better leave the horses here," Doc said. The others agreed.

They made their way to the rear of the barn on foot. All the combatants were intent on the fight, and no one spotted the three new arrivals. Standing along the back wall of the barn, Doc drew his Diamondback and checked the load. Raider shoved cartridges into the magazine of his carbine until it was full, then jacked a round into the chamber.

"There's a door over there," Raider said. "I'll go in first and see what kind of trouble I can get myself into."

He eased through the door, then stepped quickly to the side so he wouldn't be outlined against the moonlit background outside. At the far end of the long center aisle he heard a rifle shot and saw a yellow muzzle flash in the darkness. Somebody was lying on the ground up there, firing out the wide front doors of the barn.

As he started forward, the man at the front called out cautiously, "Who's there?" Raider didn't recognize the voice.

"It's Barnett," Raider mumbled, recalling the name of one of the outlaws.

"You got any spare Winchester rounds, Smiley?" the gunman asked. "I'm almost out."

"Yeah, I'll bring them up," Raider replied.

As he approached the front of the barn, choosing his steps carefully in the murky darkness, the man by the front doors fired again. Somewhere in a nearby stall, a horse snorted and pawed at the ground nervously.

"We got 'em pinned down good in that cook shack," the man said. "There's no way in hell they can get out of there without getting blasted. Who do you figure they are, Smiley? After all the killing we done up there in K.C., it wouldn't surprise me none if they were a pair of U.S. marshals." Raider smiled to himself in the darkness. That cinched it! These *were* the men who had pulled the Fidelity National robbery. He merely grunted rather than speaking again.

"Well, whoever they are, the sonsabitches sure can shoot," the man said with a trace of admiration. "Tanner's sprawled out by the stalls, dead as an anvil, and there's a couple more of our fellows down in front of the bunkhouse. I can't tell who they are from here."

A slat of moonlight spilled in through the open doors. When Raider stopped and knelt beside him, the man turned his head to look up. Raider bashed him in the face with the flat of his rifle stock before he had time to speak or act. The gunman's head dropped limply, leaking a rivulet of blood onto the Winchester he was holding.

Raider pulled the man's rifle free and slammed the barrel against a nearby support pole. Then he took the man's revolver, jammed a pinch of dirt down the muzzle, and replaced it in its hoster. If he did happen to come to, which didn't seem likely for a man in his condition, he wouldn't be much of a threat.

Raider returned to the back of the barn, stuck his head out the door, and motioned for the others to come in. The three of them went to the front doors of the barn and got their first look at the battlefield.

The main house was straight out from them about fifty yards away. Nearer on the right was a long narrow building with several windows and two separate doors along its front. To the left was a square frame building with two metal stovepipes protruding from the roof, one on either end. No lights burned in any of the buildings, but muzzle flashes were stabbing out into the night from all of them, making it difficult at first to tell who was shooting in what direction.

"Before he started his nap," Raider said, glancing down at the limp form at their feet, "this fellow told me they were pinned down in the cook shack. That must be it over there." He pointed to the building on the left. A spear of light lanced out from one of the windows as somebody fired from inside. To the rear of the cook shack two men were hunkered down behind a long watering trough, shooting toward the building. Frank and Jesse seemed to be completely surrounded by Smolett's men.

"If we let my cousins know we're here," Lucy suggested, "they might be able to make a run for this barn. Then we could take some of these horses and get away."

"Get away?" Raider exclaimed. "We came out here to get these bastards. What do we want to get away for?"

"But look," Lucy exclaimed, sweeping the field of fire with a wave of her hand.

"They've already lost four men that we know of," Raider said. "How many did you say you saw out here yesterday, Doc?"

"I saw nine, but there must be more here now," Doc said. "I counted at least eight muzzle flashes a minute ago. Two behind the cook shack, three in the bunkhouse, and three in the main house."

"That makes it eight to five, but we've still got surprise on our side," Raider said. "I say we take 'em."

"Why not?" Doc said with a shrug. "Let's go for the glory."

"Okay, here's what I've got in mind...." Raider began to explain to them.

Doc tried not to think about how much damage he was doing to his best gray suit as he crawled through the dry prairie grass, hugging the ground like a lover. A few yards behind him, Lucy followed as stealthily as a Comanche. At one point he paused and risked raising his head above the twelve-inch grass to get his bearings. Their two targets, the men behind the watering trough at the rear of the cook shack, were about fifty feet ahead. They were almost close enough. Almost . . .

One of the men ahead fired the last round in his revolver and turned to sit with his back to the trough to reload. As he did so, Doc ducked back down, trying to melt into the darkness. But he was a fraction of a second too slow. The man raised up slightly, staring into the darkness toward Doc.

"Now, Lucy!" Doc called back to the girl. As he spoke he raised back up, took careful aim with his revolver and fired two rounds. The man by the trough grunted once and settled sideways to the ground.

"Frank! Jesse!" Lucy called out loudly. "Don't shoot out the back way. It's us!" They had decided earlier that it should be she who called out the warning since the brothers would recognize her voice.

When the commotion started, the second man behind the trough turned in surprise and brought his rifle around. By then Doc was already on his feet and charging, firing the .38 as he ran. An instant later the man opened up with the rifle.

A sudden pain lanced through the lower left side of Doc's abdomen, but he had enough momentum to carry him forward another few feet. Desperately he snapped off the last couple of shots in his revolver, and finally he connected. The rifle spilled from the gunman's hands and he slumped forward, settling in a position that curiously resembled an Arab at his prayers.

A second later Doc stumbled and went down. His head was already beginning to swirl, but he fought to hold on to consciousness. A fire was blazing in his gut, and his limbs seemed to have hardly any strength left in them.

"Doc? Oh my God! Doc!"

Lucy knelt over him. Pain wrung a guttural moan from his lips as she struggled to turn him over onto his back. "Take it easy, girl!" he complained past clenched teeth.

"We've got to get out of the open!" she told him shrilly. She was close to hysterics. "We're exposed here. I've got to get you to that cook shack!"

"I don't think I can get up," Doc told her. "I'm gut shot, and I think it's bad. Real bad." A bullet chewed up a chunk of sod near his shoulder and another nipped at the tip of his left shoe. They were definitely in somebody's sights. Then suddenly, like a reprieve from the fates, the light that bathed them began to dissolve away. A drifting cloud had chosen that very opportune moment to float in front of the moon.

"Now's our chance!" Lucy said. She pulled desperately at his arm, and Doc gave her what little help he could. He managed to get onto his knees, and Lucy pulled his arm over her shoulders, straining to lift him to his feet. Bullets continued to strike all around them, but the invisible gunman was firing blindly into the darkness now.

Suddenly Doc felt strong hands grip his other arm and draw him upward. "What's the matter, Pink?" the familiar voice asked. "Are you going to let one tiny chunk of lead keep you down?"

With Frank's help, they started toward the back of the cook shack at a lumbering trot. Shots still sang by them occasionally, and at one point Doc heard Frank grunt in surprise. He stumbled slightly, then caught a new grip around Doc's waist and hurried on. They shoved through the back door of the cook shack, and Frank and Lucy deposited Doc unceremoniously on the floor.

"See what you can do for him, Lucy," Frank ordered. He was limping as he moved off to resume his position at one of the back windows. Soon the moonlight swept over the landscape again, and by its light Frank began to dress the deep bullet crease on his left thigh.

"What happened with you two?" Lucy asked as she began

peeling away Doc's jacket and shirt to get to his wound. Doc was lapsing in and out of consciousness, fighting against the repeated waves of pain.

"I guess Smolett's smarter than we gave him credit for," Frank admitted. "He had sense enough to keep sentries posted around the place, and one of them spotted us before we saw him."

"We were slipping across to the main house when the bastard opened up on us," Jesse said from across the room. "We couldn't tell where he was, so we ducked in here. A couple of minutes later all hell broke loose. For the first few minutes it was like being in the Alamo, but after we dropped a few of them, they got more cautious."

"All of them took to cover finally, and that's how it's been for the past half hour or so," Frank said. "I guess they figured on waiting us out."

"Where's his friend?" Jesse asked, nodding his head toward Doc. "Dead?"

"I hope not," Lucy said. "They came up with a plan. Doc and I were supposed to come around behind this place and get to you while Raider circled around to take on the men in the bunkhouse. Then, if all that worked, we were supposed to charge the main house together."

"If that isn't a stupid goddamn idea, then I never heard one," Jesse scoffed. "Pinkertons! Shit!"

"Yeah, I guess they weren't smart like you two, were they, Jesse?" Lucy snapped. She heard Frank chuckling in the darkness.

"What low station have we reached, brother," Frank reflected stoically, "when we need a couple of Pinkerton dicks to pull our irons from the fire?"

"If you ever tell Cole or Charlie or any of the others in the gang about this," Jesse growled, "I swear I'll beat you to death, Frank."

• • •

Raider knelt at the window at the rear of the bunkhouse, scanning the dark interior. It didn't take him long to locate the positions of the three men inside by the flash of their weapons. Two were stationed at front windows toward the left end of the building, and the third was kneeling by one of the front doors. All were gazing out toward the cook shack and paying no attention to anything behind them.

Raider moved along the rear of the building until he was standing outside the back door. Holding the carbine in his left hand, he drew his revolver with his right and checked the load. His heart was thudding heavily, filling his chest with its drumbeats. He drew two deep breaths to calm himself and tried not to think about death.

His first kick blasted the door open as if from an explosion. Raider burst into the room with his weapons ready. He already knew where his first target would be. The man kneeling by the door tried to swing his rifle around, but he didn't get it down in time. Raider killed him with the pistol, then spun left and dropped into a kneeling position. The man at the nearest window was able to get one shot off, but it was fired in panic and went wild. Raider fired twice, watched his target double up, and readjusted his aim toward the third gunman.

The instincts of the lone survivor were better than those of his dead companions. While Raider was occupied killing his friends, the man dropped flat on the floor and rolled out of the revealing moonlight that came in through the window. His first shot furrowed the stock of Raider's carbine and the second nicked at the brim of his hat. Firing frantically at the man's muzzle flashes, Raider emptied the last three rounds from his revlover without connecting.

Raider heard a low chuckle from the far side of the bunkhouse. "That's six, son of a bitch!" a deep voice announced in triumph. There was a shuffling sound and a form rose into view near the window.

Raider couldn't believe it. *The ignorant bastard actually*

wanted to gloat awhile before he fired the fatal bullet!

"You mean to tell me you haven't heard of the new seven-shooters?" Raider asked as he raised the carbine at his side, holding it like a pistol. The man didn't see the rifle as he started toward Raider.

"You're fulla crap." The gunman laughed. "There ain't no such a thing." He was enjoying his moment of triumph so much that he was getting careless. Against Raider, such errors were frequently fatal.

Raider aimed as carefully as he could and pulled the trigger. The rifle bullet spattered into the man's midsection, hurling him back. His legs gave way beneath him and he sprawled onto the floor. Raider rushed over and kicked the man's pistol out of reach, then stood looking down at his bearded features. The dying man's eyes were filled with wonderment and disbelief.

"Dumb shit," Raider said before turning away.

Jesse knelt by the front window, staring cautiously toward the bunkhouse. "The shooting's stopped over there," he told the others.

Lucy had Doc's shirt off and was using a strip torn from a curtain to swab the blood away and examine the wound. Only a moment before, Doc's eyes had rolled upward and his eyelids sagged shut as unconsciousness claimed him. At least she hoped it was only unconsciousness.

"So Raider either got all of them," Frank said, "or they got him."

"It don't matter much to me which way it turned out," Jesse commented.

"If they had killed Raider, they'd be shooting at us again, wouldn't they?" Lucy asked hopefully.

"Maybe," Jesse said, giving her scant encouragement.

A long minute passed, then they heard a shrill whistle from the direction of the bunkhouse. "That's him," Lucy announced with open relief. "That's Raider's signal. He's ready to start for the main house."

Jesse turned and gazed across the room toward his brother. "How about it, Frank?" he asked."

"Well, we came here to even the score with Smolett, and that's probably where he is," Frank said. "Chances are, that's where the money is too."

"What about your leg?"

"I can get by on it for a while longer. I've got the bleeding almost stopped," Frank said. He rose to his feet and started toward the door, walking with a limp.

Before leaving, Jesse turned to his cousin and said, "You'd better stay here, Lucy. If things go bad for us over there, you head back to where you left your horse and get out of here. Don't worry about that damn Pinkerton. Gut shot like that, he's probably a dead man anyway." Lucy simply nodded when she heard the instructions.

Raider was kneeling just outside one of the front doors of the bunkhouse when he saw Frank and Jesse James come out of the cook shack. Frank signaled with his revolver to Raider, then pointed it toward the main house about thirty yards away. The three of them started cautiously forward. It alarmed Raider to see that Doc wasn't with the two brothers. He realized immediately what that must mean, but there wasn't time to go check on his partner. More pressing business needed taking care of first.

The first shot from the house singed Raider's shirt between his right arm and his ribs. He hit the ground like a stone, then crawled frantically forward toward the cover of a pile of lumber. The men in the house threw out a heavy volley that peppered the lumber like raindrops. Raider glanced to the left and saw that the James brothers had disappeared. They were probably circling, he thought.

Raider rose to a squat behind the lumber, and when the shooting let up for an instant, he sprinted forward. Running in a zigzag pattern, he made for the back porch of the house. Bullets filled the air around him again almost immediately, but when he reached the porch, he made a dive and rolled under it.

He was so close now that he smelled the gunsmoke from the guns of his opponents and heard them yelling at one another inside. They seemed to realize that they were the only survivors from the entire crew, and the fact that they were now the ones under seige was making them desperate.

"Who are you?" someone shouted angrily from inside. "Damn you anyway? What do you want from us?"

Raider wasn't inclined to answer, but from somewhere off in the darkness, Jesse couldn't resist the opportunity. "Only your lives, Smolett!" he shouted back. "That's what we want!"

"Who the hell are you?" the man inside repeated.

"We're old friends of yours, Hank," Frank intoned. "Old friends with an old debt that needs settling. Remember up in Independence when you led us into that Yankee ambush?"

"Frank? my God! Is that you and Jesse out there?"

"None other. And since you've decided to go around impersonating us lately," Frank went on, "we figure we deserve a cut from your last bank job in Kansas City, too."

"You can have a cut, Frank," Smolett promised. "You can have half. I'll throw it out to you."

"But we also want your ass, Hank," Jesse said. "We want all of that!"

Raider could tell that the brothers were continuing to move as they spoke, easing farther around the side of the house. They were positioning themselves to attack. He crawled down to one end of the porch, cocked the hammer of his revolver, and waited. Above he could hear heavy footfalls as Smolett and his men readjusted their positions.

"Look, you fellows can have all the money," Smolett offered desperately. "Couldn't we just forget about something that happened that long ago? It was a war, for Christ's sake! Everybody was making mistakes! But you made it through all right. You didn't get killed that night." He paused, but received no response.

"Frank? What do you say?" Smolett tried again. "Take all the money and leave me be. Most of it's still left. There's enough to make a man forget a lot of old grudges. So what do you say, Frank? Jesse?" Neither answered. Raider sensed that the time was near.

When the first shots sounded from the far side of the house, Raider leaped onto the porch. He fired two rounds through the closest window, then sprang forward and went crashing through the opening into what proved to be a kitchen. A man lay on his back just inside the window. He was holding the right side of his chest with both hands and blood was gushing out between his fingers. Raider started to shoot him instinctively, then decided not to waste the bullet. He kicked the man's shotgun across the room, then turned to a doorway that led to an adjoining dining room. From the front of the house he heard muffled shots and the sound of somebody running.

Raider sprang into the dining room, but found it empty. Beside two windows there were dozens of spent shell casings, indicating that this was where at least two of Smolett's men had been during a major portion of the gunfight. But apparently they had fled when they realized they were about to be attacked.

Another shot roared from the front, and a man screamed in agony. A second shot ended his wails. The James boys weren't taking prisoners.

Raider met the brothers in a long hallway that led from the front door to the dining room. "Did we get them all?" he asked as he shoved a couple of fresh cartridges into his revolver. He noted that Frank was bleeding from a fresh wound on his arm, but he still appeared to be in reasonably good shape.

"We haven't seen Smolett," Jesse said. "Did you get him back there?"

"I plugged one bastard," Raider said, "but there wasn't time for no introductions. Maybe it's him."

When they reached the kichen, Jesse went over and checked the downed man. By then, most of the life had already bled out of the wounded gunman. He gazed up at Jesse with glazed, expressionless eyes.

"Goddamn it, that's not him either," Jesse announced furiously. "Where in the hell did the son of a bitch go?"

"He's probably hiding somewhere here in the house," Raider said. "We'll have to search the place room by room, and then if we still don't find him—"

"I've got the girl, Frank!"

The shouted warning came from outside behind the house. Raider's blood froze in his veins.

CHAPTER FIFTEEN

Smolett was standing outside the front door of the cook shack, holding the muzzle of a pistol under Lucy's chin. His other arm was wrapped around her chest, holding her body in front of his. He had a pair of saddlebags, which probably contained the money from the bank robbery, thrown over his shoulder.

"You know I won't mind blowing her fucking brains out if I have to," Smolett sneered at them. Raider and the two brothers stood in the kitchen, staring out at them helplessly.

"We know that, Hank," Frank answered calmly. "I guess now its our turn to ask you what you want."

"Ever since the war, you two have thought you were such hot shit," Smolett shouted at them. "A pair of real big-time bad men. Well, I guess you know now who the better man is, don't you? Don't you, Frank?"

"It looks like you're the better man, Smolett," Frank called out to him. "You sure got the best of us this time."

"I think I could drop him from here with my rifle," Raider suggested quietly to the others.

"No. We're not risking Lucy's life," Frank told him. "We'll play it his way for a little while and see what happens." Raider agreed. He really didn't like the idea of risking Lucy's life that way any more than they did.

"You see, boys," Smolett explained to them, "the old fart who built that house forty years ago was mortally scared of Indians. He was sure that someday they'd raid the ranch and burn the house down on top of him. So he dug himself a tunnel. It leads from a secret entrance inside the house over to a trapdoor in the floor of the cook shack. Don't you wish you'd knowed about that when we had you pinned down?"

"That's pretty clever, Hank," the elder James admitted. His tone remained calm throughout. He didn't want to do or say anything that would make Smolett pull that trigger. "But now that you're holding all the cards, what is it that you want?"

"I'm leaving now with the money," Smolett said, "and I'm taking this little cunt, whoever she is, with me. I assume she's valuable enough to you that you don't want to see her killed. If I get the slightest hint that any of you are trying to follow me, this bitch is in real trouble. I might start leaving pieces of her lying around for you to track me by."

By that time, Jesse was ready to explode with helpless rage. His brother glanced at him, assayed his mood, and cautioned him, "Don't start getting impulsive on us, Jesse. You know the crazy bastard means what he says."

"I know, Frank," Jesse hissed. "Goddamn it, I remember what he's like. But once he lets her go, this country won't be big enough for the son of a bitch to hide in."

"I'm leaving now," Smolett said. "You'd best remember

what I said, unless you want to see this bitch die a piece at a time."

They remained where they were, watching as Smolett made his way across the open area to the barn. He kept himself shielded behind Lucy the entire time, and there was nothing any of them could do except wait. In a couple of minutes Smolett came riding out of the barn, holding the reins of a second horse on which Lucy was mounted. He had her hands bound in front of her and tied to the saddle horn between her knees. They disappeared in the darkness before Raider could bring his rifle up and get a clear shot at him.

"It's time to figure out what we do next," Frank said.

"That's easy enough," Jesse said. "I'm going after them."

"Okay, I'm with you," Frank said. "But we'll have to give them a decent lead to start out with. Let him think he's actually going to make it."

"You're too shot up to go, Frank," Jesse said. "You've caught two slugs already, and we both know that by morning you'd just be holding me back." Frank agreed reluctantly to what his brother said.

"Well, I haven't got any holes in me," Raider said. "I'm going, but first I've got to check on Doc."

As they left the house, Jesse told Raider, "Your partner looked like hell when we left him, and Smolett probably finished him if he wasn't dead already. But you can check. I'll go out and bring my horse and Frank's in. We won't find anything better to ride around this place."

In the cook shack, Raider knelt by Doc's side while Frank lit a lamp. Doc did look like hell. His features were as white as paper, and he was lying in an enormous pool of his own blood. The bandage Lucy had improvised for his wound was saturated with blood.

"It looks bad for him, don't it?" Raider said, glancing up at Frank in despair. "Damn it all to hell, I think he's dead already."

During all the time that the two of them had been partners, both had realized that someday such a moment as this would arrive. Men didn't face death day after day, month after month, like the two of them did without knowing deep inside that in the end a bullet would be their only reward for their years of service in a thankless profession. But it wasn't a matter that they ever talked about, and it wasn't something that a man could ever fully prepare himself for. Raider felt a lump about the size of a goose egg rise in his throat. He couldn't quite envision a world without his close friend in it.

At first he wasn't sure whether he had actually seen Doc's chest move or whether his desperate desire for his friend to still be alive had made him imagine it. Eagerly he probed at Doc's throat with his fingertips and finally located a faint pulse.

"I can feel it!" he exclaimed to Frank. "His heart's still pumping. Come on, Doc! Fight for it! Live, damn you!"

They heard the sound of horses outside, and Jesse called out, "Hey, Pink! You coming?"

"I can take care of him as well as you can," Frank said. "You might as well go." Raider looked up at the outlaw, an unspoken question in his eyes. "I know all you've got to go on is my word for that," Frank told him. "I guess what it all boils down to is whether or not you can trust me after all this time. You decide."

Raider rose slowly and turned to Frank. "The main thing now is to plug the hole and get the bleeding stopped," he instructed.

"I've taken care of a gunshot or two in my day," the outlaw assured him. "I know what to do."

"There'll be a posse along from town in a little while, and they can get him in to see a doctor. But don't worry. They won't know who you are, so there shouldn't be any trouble. Just drop out of sight the first chance you get."

"I can handle that, too," Frank said.

"Damn it, Pink! Are you coming or not?" Jesse called

impatiently to Raider. "While you're in there fiddledy-fart-
ing around, that asshole Smolett is putting more ground
between us and him."

"When you get him, Raider," Frank said solemnly. "You
make sure he pays." Raider nodded and turned toward the
door.

Despite the animosities between them, Raider had to
admit to himself that he and Jesse James made a good team.
The outlaw was a skillful tracker, as good as Raider himself
on his best day. Despite the darkness, they were able to
stay on Smolett and Lucy's trail throughout the night.

Smolett was headed southwest, back toward Texas. It
was country that he would be familiar with, and an area
where a man could easily disappear without a trace. The
money he was carrying would guarantee that he could live
the good life for a long time in the frontier regions of Texas
and Mexico. But Raider and Jesse were determined to fix
things so that Smolett didn't have the chance to live any
sort of life anywhere.

They reached the Walnut River at daybreak, and as they
were preparing to cross, Raider noticed a small swatch of
cloth hung on a briar. He pointed it out to Jesse, and both
of them dismounted to have a look.

"It's a piece from Lucy's shirt," Raider said. "Remember
she had that red plaid shirt on last night?"

"The girl's sure no fool," Jesse said. "And look here.
Something's written in the dirt." The letters "OKMU" were
scratched in the sandy dirt beneath the strip of cloth.

"It has to be some kind of message," Raider said. "But
what do you figure she meant by it? 'Okmu?' Could it be
the name of a place, or some kind of Indian word maybe?"

"I don't see any reason why she would use any Indian
words," Jesse said. "But I know this part of the country
pretty well, and I've never heard of anyplace called Okmu."

Raider   sounded   the   letters   out   individually.

"O...K...M...U. She could be trying to tell us she's okay. But what about the rest? Are they the initials of someplace?"

"What if she didn't get to finish writing?" Jesse suggested.

"Sure, that makes sense. She's okay and they're going to someplace that starts with 'mu.'"

"Mulvane!" Jesse exclaimed. "It's a little town a few miles due west of here. But I'm not sure how much good it's going to do us to know what town they're riding toward. It's not going to help us get her out of this mess alive."

"It might, James," Raider said.

"How's that?"

"If we know where they're going, then we don't necessarily have to stay behind them anymore, do we? We could ride ahead."

A light of understanding showed in Jesse's eyes. "I see what you're getting at," he said. "Since Smolett's so goddamn fond of ambushes, it wouldn't be such a bad idea to set one up for him. It sure wouldn't be something he'd expect."

"So let's ride for Mulvane," Raider said, urging his horse down the embankment and into the river.

After nearly two hours of hard riding, Raider began to fully appreciate the strength and stamina of his borrowed mount. But it just made sense, he figured, that men such as Frank and Jesse James, whose lives frequently depended on the quality of the horseflesh beneath them, would be mounted on only the best.

During one brief rest stop, Raider turned to Jesse and commented, "This here's about the finest horse I've ever been astraddle. Did you and your brother buy these animals or steal them?"

Jesse turned to Raider with a sour look on his face and asked, "Would you believe the truth if you heard it?"

"Try me."

"All right. The fact is, I raised them on my farm. My boy and I raised them up from colts, and Frank and I trained them."

"On your farm?" Raider asked. "It's hard to come up with a picture of a gunslinger like you pushing a plow and tending livestock."

"Look, Pink," Jesse replied. "Last year the James Gang got blamed for upwards of half a dozen robberies, but we actually only pulled two of them. They took maybe two weeks apiece to plan and pull off. What in the blazes did you think we did with the rest of our time? Sit around picking our noses and putting a polish on our forty-fives?"

"I never thought much about it," Raider admitted. "But it's just hard to imagine owlhoots like you and your brother living like real people."

"You can just drop the 'owlhoot' bullshit," Jesse warned, swinging back up into the saddle. "If you have to call me anything, my real name will do just fine."

"Then you might keep in mind that I got a name too," Raider said, "and it ain't the color of whore's bloomers."

They decided to set up their ambush on a hill a few miles east of the town of Mulvane. Considering the expanses of open range land that were common in this area, it was the best location they could come up with on short notice.

The road to Mulvane came straight in from the east, detouring briefly around the base of the hill before resuming its straight, monotonous course. A few cottonwoods lined the road and the slopes of the hill, providing them with the necessary cover for what they planned to do. They knew there were no guarantees that Smolett would ride this way, but if their guess was right and he was headed for Mulvane, the route seemed logical. It was a gamble with Lucy's life as the stakes, but it was one which they both knew they had to make.

"All right, I'll be in the trees up there on the slope so I

can spot them in plenty of time," Raider said. "I'll let them get on into the trees, but when they reach that little clearing directly below the hill, I'll drop Smolett out of the saddle with my carbine. You can be hiding down near the clearing. If I only wound him with my first shot, you'll be close by to make sure he doesn't have a chance to hurt Lucy."

"Most of that sounds fine to me," Jesse said, "except for one thing. That's my cousin this asshole's got with him, and I want to make sure the man behind the rifle is the best there is. *I'll* be up on the slope, and *you'll* be hiding down by the clearing. That's the way it's going to work."

Raider started to argue, then decided not to bother. If there was one thing in the world he ought to be able to trust Jesse James to do properly, it was to kill a man. It didn't matter who was where, just so long as Smolett was killed and Lucy was not. Saving her life was all that counted now.

Once they were in position, they didn't have long to wait. From behind a thick cottonwood alongside the road where he was waiting, Raider heard Jesse's bobwhite call from up the hill and knew that the riders were in sight. He drew his pistol from the holster, thumbed the hammer back and waited with his back flattened against the tree. When he began to hear the sound of two horses approaching he tensed, but didn't try to look around. The first move was Jesse's.

As they neared the clearing, one of the horses seemed to detect Raider's presence nearby. He heard the animal snort nervously, then Smolett muttered, "What's the matter boy? You smell something up there?" Smolett stopped his mount, and Raider clearly heard the click of a pistol being cocked. As the seconds passed, Raider decided that Smolett must be just out of Jesse's line of sight.

Then finally Raider heard Smolett say, "Here, woman. You take your own reins and ride ahead of me for a spell. But don't try to pull nothing. I'll have this Colt aimed at the center of your back all the way."

A panicky sort of feeling invaded Raider's gut. His instincts began to tell him that the whole thing was turning sour. Things weren't going at all according to plan, and he sensed that the whole mess was about to blow up in their face like a hot jar of home brew.

When the shot roared out from up on the hillside, Raider spun around from behind his cover with his pistol ready. To his dismay, he saw that Smolett was still in the saddle and that Lucy was in between them so that it was impossible to get a clear shot. The only thing that was keeping Smolett from shooting them both was the violent rearing of his horse.

As Raider leaped into the edge of the road and Lucy dug her heels into her horse's sides, trying to get clear, Jesse fired a second shot with his rifle. Raider danced out of the way of the flying hooves of Lucy's mount, then raised his revolver, hoping for a shot at Smolett. Too late he realized that Jesse's second bullet had struck Smolett's horse and that the animal was toppling in his direction. Raider dug in his heels and stumbled clumsily backward, trying to avoid being crushed by the falling animal.

The outlaw was thrown clear as his horse went down, and he crashed heavily into Raider. They rolled back into the brush in a tangled heap, and both lost their weapons in the confusion. But Smolett had an immediate edge over Raider. He had a second pistol stuck down in the waistband of his pants.

As his opponent pulled the weapon out, Raider made a grab for it with his left hand and crashed his right fist into the other man's face. Smolett roared in anger and pain, still trying to bring the gun to bear on Raider, but Raider had the advantages of weight and power over him. Raider drew his fist back again and delivered a powerful blow to the outlaw's throat.

It took Smolett a moment to realize the seriousness of his problem. He struggled on for another few seconds, but when his crushed windpipe refused to pass any air into his lungs, his fingers let go of the gun and began to claw and tear at his throat desperately. Raider picked up the pistol, then drew away and watched in amazement.

It wasn't the easiest way in the world for a man to die. Smolett's face grew progressively redder, and after a couple of minutes the color deepened to awesome shades of purple and blue. The doomed outlaw writhed around on the ground like a headless snake, snatching senselessly at the air and issuing guttural gags and grunts. Eventually his body weakened and his movements slowed. He died with a final reflexive jerk that arched his entire torso several inches off the ground and then dropped him back suddenly.

"The sorry bastard," Jesse commented from several feet away. Raider had been so absorbed in watching Smolett die that he hadn't even noticed Jesse coming down the hillside. Casually Jesse raised the muzzle of his rifle and fired one shot. Smolett's head exploded as if a charge had been placed inside it.

"Why couldn't you do that a while ago?" Raider complained bitterly. "First his goddamn horse almost crushes me to death, and then this bastard decides he's got to fall out of the saddle right on top of me. Then he almost blasted me with this second six-shooter he had stuck down in his britches. Tell me all about how you're the best shot there is, James!"

"It couldn't be helped," Jesse said. "First Lucy was in my line of sight, and then his horse started rearing up and dancing all over the place."

Lucy's horse had run several hundred yards down the road before she regained control of it, but finally she came riding back to them. Jesse took out a folding knife to cut the ropes that bound her wrists, and she slid tiredly to the ground.

"Anyway," Jesse said, continuing the argument with Raider, "it don't seem like it would have made much difference if you got it from Smolett. It would've just meant

that you died a few minutes earlier than you're going to."
When Raider looked around, he saw that Jesse had the rifle
aimed at him. "Pass the gun over real careful," Jesse instructed him.

"I should've figured this," Raider said as he surrendered
the revolver he had taken from Smolett. "You can pretend
all you want, but when it comes right down to apples and
oranges, your kind hasn't got honor enough to fill my gran-
ny's thimble."

"What's honor got to do with it?" Jesse scoffed. "I stuck
by my part of the bargain all the way. I didn't raise a finger
against you while we were going after Smolett and his
bunch, but the last one of them is dead now and all deals
are off. And you're still a fucking Pinkerton."

To one side, Lucy was watching them with shock and
disbelief. Jesse handed her his rifle, but continued to cover
Raider with the pistol. "Is the money in those saddlebags
Smolett had, Lucy?" he asked.

She answered quietly that it was.

"All right, get the money, get on your horse, and ride a
little ways back down the road," he instructed her. "I doubt
if you'll want to stay around to see what's going to happen
here."

"You can't, Jesse," Lucy told him.

"Listen, gal," Jesse told her coldly. "This man is a Pinkerton, and all we've been through in the past few days
doesn't change the fact that the lousy Pinkertons killed my
and Frank's little brother and crippled our mama. They did
it, and they'll go on paying for it as long as I've got the
strength left in me to pull a trigger."

"Do you really have that much hate in you, Jesse?" Lucy
asked in wonderment. "You've ridden with this man and
you've fought alongside him for a good reason. Even though
you don't like him, I think you know in your heart that he
deserves to live. Just five minutes ago he risked his life to
save mine. What am I supposed to think about that now

that you're about to kill him? What do you think about what he just did?"

"I'm not about to plead with the likes of you to spare my life," Raider told the outlaw. "But I will tell you this. If you pull that trigger, it'll be the biggest mistake you ever made."

"Will you kill a man simply because of a name, Jesse?" Lucy asked.

As Jesse James slowly lowered the barrel of the revolver, he looked Raider in the eye and said, "Mister, you sure live a charmed life. Every time I've tried to drop a hammer on you, one of my own kin has started flapping their jaw and talked me out of it. Seems like I'd better just give up trying."

"This time it was a smarter decision than you know," Raider told him. "Take a close look at that gun you're holding."

Jesse examined the weapon, then looked up at Raider in surprise. "Looks like I'd of had myself a handful of dynamite," he said.

"I stuck the mud down that barrel myself, and I noticed it as soon as you drew down on me," Raider told him. "Smolett must have picked it up when he went in the barn to get the horses." As casually as he could manage, Raider walked over and retrieved his own revolver from where it lay on the ground near Smolett's body. Then, turning back to Jesse, he added, "And by the way, I'm taking the money back with me."

A rare grin crept over Jesse's features. "All right, Raider," he said. "I guess my brother and I can always find someplace to get some of our own."

CHAPTER SIXTEEN

Nellie was sitting beside Doc's bed spooning vegetable soup into him when Raider entered the room. She had scarcely left his side for a moment since the time two days before when the posse returned him to Dulcinda half dead in the back of a wagon. The town doctor may have been the one who patched up the hole in Doc's body, but it was Nellie's tender care that was doing the most to bring about his quick recovery.

The smile on Doc's face, weak though it might be, was a heartening sight to Raider. He could still vividly recall the feelings of emptiness and loss he had experienced during that one terrible moment when he believed his partner was dead, and he resolved that from now on he was going to begin showing Doc more consideration and appreciation.

"You're looking better by the hour, Doc," Raider said as he came to the side of the bed. "When are you going to get your tail out of that bed and start helping me with all this paperwork?" Resolves were fine, but he didn't want Doc to start getting spoiled.

"Good heavens, Raider!" Nellie said, hurrying to defend her patient. "He's so weak he can hardly lift a spoon by himself, and you want him to go back to work?"

Raider surveyed his partner with a critical eye and noted, "He's been worse off, and so have I. But that never stops Allan Pinkerton from demanding that we fill out twenty-five different reports and case journals the minute the last owlhoot falls to the ground. And he always wants them submitted the day before yesterday."

"Obviously you've just come from a meeting with him," Doc commented.

"I think old age is softening him up some, Doc," Raider said. "After he got done bawling me out again for the way we handled this case, he actually admitted that we did a good job. And he asked how you were doing. How are you doing, Doc? Really."

"There's been times in my life when I've felt better than I do right now," Doc admitted. "But there's also been times when I was laid up and didn't receive near the kind of care that I'm getting this time." Nellie smiled and shoved a spoonful of soup at him.

"Do you feel good enough to talk? There's a couple of things we've got to get straight between us," Raider said. "I've been giving the old man the runaround about some of what went on, but pretty soon I'm going to have to tell him one complete story and stick to it. And the story we all tell had better be the same."

"Meaning we've got to decide who those men were that helped us?" Doc asked.

"And why they helped."

"What have you told him so far?"

"Well, I gave him the names B. J. Woodson and Thomas Howard, and I told him we hooked up with them over in Caseyville. But I said you're the one that located them and that you knew more about them than I did. It was the best stall I could think of."

"Whatever story we work up, it's going to have to be airtight if we plan to slip it by Allan Pinkerton and Wagner. They'll latch onto any discrepancies in a second. I'll need some time to think about it."

"What in the world are you two talking about?" Nellie interrupted at last. "This conversation isn't making a bit of sense to me."

"We're talking about what to say regarding those two men who helped us on this case," Doc told her simply.

"Well, why do you keep saying 'those two men'? For heaven's sake! Those two men just happened to be Frank and Jesse James, the two most notorious outlaws in the United States!" She looked back and forth from one of them to the other with a growing sense of alarm. "I've been working on my account of all of this during the times when you were alseep, Doc, and I've almost got it ready. I plan to wire it to the *Times* today."

"You might have to make a few changes before you send it out," Doc suggested.

"No dice, Doc," Nellie said firmly. "Even if this wasn't the biggest story of my career, I couldn't let even you censor my work."

"How do you know for sure those men were Frank and Jesse James?" Raider asked her. "They said they were, but they also used the names Woodson and Howard. Maybe that's who they really were."

"You two are trying to pull a fast one on me for some reason," she said angrily. "But I'm not going to let you get away with it. This is the biggest story of my life. It can *make* my career in newspapers!"

"No matter what you call our two accomplices," Doc told her gently, "it's still a pretty good story. Good enough to land you that reporter's job, I'm sure. But the problem here is all the complications that would arise if we admit that we spent that much time around Frank and Jesse James and never once tried to apprehend them. It would cause a scandal that might ruin the agency, and when the blame started filtering down, Allan Pinkerton would want to have the both of us drawn and quartered. We might even be arrested for aiding and abetting known criminals, or something of the sort."

"I'm really sorry about all of that," Nellie said. "I wouldn't want to see either of you in such trouble. But how can I let a story like this get past me? How could I do that?"

"It looks like you're going to have to," Raider said. He put a consoling hand on her shoulder, but she shrugged away from him and stood up. She went to the window and stood with her back to the two men as Raider continued. "We won't back you up," he said. "We couldn't. And after we file our reports, Allan Pinkerton will tell the world you're off your rocker if you claim two of his men worked with the James brothers to solve the Fidelity National Bank robbery."

"I'd look like a fool," Nellie said. From the sound of her voice, they could tell she was crying. When she turned to the door, Raider tried to stop her, but she shoved past him and went out. Raider turned back to Doc and shrugged.

"I'd delayed discussing this with her," Doc said, "because I figured it might be the end of all this good nursing I've been getting."

"And the end of everything else too, probably."

"I'll give her all the information I can for her story after she cools down a little," Doc said, staring at the door. "Life goes on."

"And so does the bullshit," Raider grumbled. "You ought to see the list of things the old man disallowed from our expense vouchers. For ten cents, I'd quit this damn outfit and get into some decent line of work, Doc. I swear I would."

"Hand me my trousers from the chair over there, Rade," Doc said. "I'll see if I've got any change."

J.D. HARDIN

"THE MOST EXCITING WESTERN WRITER SINCE LOUIS L'AMOUR"
—JAKE LOGAN

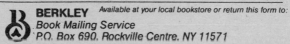

JAKE LOGAN

Prices may be slightly higher in Canada.

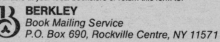